WORLDS OF IF

BY

Bruce Pierce

ISBN # Softcover 9798406245491

This is a work of fiction. Names, characters, places and incidents either are the product of the author's imagination or are used fictitiously, and any resemblance to any actual persons, living or dead, events, or locales is entirely coincidental.

This book was printed in the United States of America.

DEDICATION

For Sherry

TABLE OF CONTENTS

1—FLYING MACHINE

"I didn't ask to be in this world," Craig Harrison stated for the record. "But you won't hear me registering any complaints."

Rance Collier gazed at two moons in the evening sky. "None of us asked to be here," he replied. "But being in this world sure beats pushing up daisies. I can tell you that much."

"Ah, but you see," said Craig, "I was on the mainland, hundreds of miles away, when the islands blew up. I wouldn't have died with the rest of you."

"I didn't know that, *amigo*. The star hoppers must've wanted you bad."

"Yeah, they must've, because they pulled me out of a moving vehicle in the dead of night."

"You were driving when they nabbed you?"

"Yeah, I sometimes wonder what happened to my Honda. I was doing seventy on an Interstate."

"I'll be jiggered. That seems awful irresponsible of the star hoppers."

"Yeah, it does, doesn't it?"

"I have to tell you, though, that I do get a kick out of the twenty-six-hour days here. It's nice to get an extra hour of sleep."

"And a three-hundred-day year is okay, too."

"Even though it reckons out, hour-wise, to eleven years here, being the same as ten years on Earth."

"Yeah, but who's counting?"

"Affirmative, *amigo*."

"How is your lovely bride?"

Rance scowled. "Aleesa is in a snit."

"What about?"

"She reckons her damsels expended too much effort working on Andy's aerial dingus."

"Yeah, maybe they did. But it's not as though the ladies have to do much hunting anymore. And they gained plenty of valuable goods in return for their services. It was a real bargain for them. They came out ahead on the deal, if you ask me."

"I can't wrangle with that reckoning, *amigo*. But it's more that Aleesa's younger sisters are lusting after those boys yonder."

"Come on. Vik and Sluggo are freshly minted teenagers."

"Affirmative, *amigo*. But they look like Adonis and Apollo."

"Yeah, they do get a lot of exercise."

"At least the boys are spending the night on the plains in tents."

"And I told their folks I'd look after them."

"Ah, that's why you're out here. You're keeping them under surveillance."

"Yeah, not that there's anything to surveil. Vik and Sluggo are scared of girls. And, up until now, the only females they'd known were their moms and Doctor Johnson and Dora. And Dora always wore her T-shirt on our visits to Earth Town."

"Where is Dora, by the way? Why isn't she out here with you?"

"She's keeping company with Aleesa and Gloria. They're watching the girls. They don't want Vik and Sluggo interacting with nearly naked nymphs."

"Okay, let me get this straight. Andy designs the dingus. And these boys assemble it."

"Vik and Sluggo did much of the designing, too. To hear them talk, Andy is just along for the ride."

"Andy is taking the boys with him?"

"He couldn't keep them from going."

"And their folks didn't kick up a fuss?"

"What could they say? It's not that Vik and Sluggo are spoiled, exactly. But they do get whatever they want."

"It works out that way, doesn't it?"

"But Andy was read the riot act about keeping them safe."

“Do you reckon he can keep them safe?”

“If I were religious, I’d be praying for it.”

“This whole business is rather reckless, you know.”

“Yeah, I know. But it would be nice to find out more about this planet.”

“The star hoppers aren’t talking to you?”

“Nope, we’re on our own.”

“Not entirely.”

“What do you mean?”

“You know what I mean. Whenever someone mentions to you that they want something or need something, a day or two later, you show up with that very thing.”

Craig winked. “I know a guy.”

“Some guy. Any possibility you could introduce me someday?”

“Yeah, maybe, I’ll see what I can do.”

“I’m not all-fired convinced that the wicker these damsels have been weaving will hold up under wind and rain, and who knows what else will be up there.”

“Dora says the wicker is durable stuff. The sisterhood makes their huts out of it, you know.”

“Affirmative, *amigo.* But those huts are protected by trees. They’ve never had to withstand a big blow. Up in the air, Andy and the boys will be buffeted about and at the mercy of the elements.”

"Andy knows that. He'll inspect every nook and cranny. That man leaves nothing to chance."

"I hear Andy got this loony whim of his from reading Jules Verne."

"Yeah, *Robur the Conqueror.* Not my favorite Jules Verne story. But it was an intriguing plot contrivance for that age."

"Affirmative, *amigo.* That age, being two centuries ago."

"This flying machine might work, though. It's a solar-powered multi-rotor, with vertical helicopter blades for lift, and horizontal propellers for going forward and backward."

"The dingus can go in reverse?"

"Yeah, if need be. Andy says he wants to get out of trouble as quickly as he got into it. And he's tacked on a few tweaks to the primary concept. The doors and windows slide open and shut, for example."

"Then, the fuselage parts were stacked out there, before the boys arrived today?"

"Yeah, Vik and Sluggo lashed up the wicker panels this afternoon. And they'll drive them to Earth Town tomorrow. They borrowed Roy's dune buggy and attached a couple of wagons to it, one behind the other."

"They got all of that stuff onto two wagons?"

"Yeah, but it'll be slow-going tomorrow. I'm going to run behind them and make certain they don't get into trouble."

"All the way to the whistle-stop?"

"I promised their parents."

"And back at the whistle-stop, they're putting together the rest of the dingus?"

"Yeah, Andy has Roy and Barney and George assisting him."

"That makes sense. George is a blacksmith, by trade. And Roy is a mechanic. And Barney is a machinist."

"And Andy used to be a machinist, himself."

"And everyone else is helping out, too?"

"Yeah, it'll take a few days to get everything done. And after that, they'll make a flight test around the valley."

"And if the test goes well?"

"Then, they'll fly the airship above the mountains and explore, what I conjecture to be, an island."

"How do you reckon this is an island?"

"You know I've encountered salt water."

"Affirmative."

"And I've seen indications of plate tectonics."

"Affirmative: The mountain formations and the raised plateau we live on."

"Yeah, and there are a few other geological indicators. But, for now, it's a hypothesis. Andy and Vik and Sluggo will find out for certain."

"I reckon this idea is ill-conceived, especially with two teenagers along. And those boys are in their early teens. They just had their thirteenth and fourteenth birthdays."

"But you'll have to admit that Vic and Sluggo are pretty mature for their ages. And they're no dummies."

"Affirmative, Dan told me the boys are always in the library, when they're not exercising or helping their folks."

"Yeah, Vik and Sluggo are dependable fellows. And they're champing at the bit for a quest."

"What are they going to do about food and water?"

"Andy will have antelope and venison jerky on board, together with nuts and seeds and legumes and dried fruit and dried vegetables. And he expects to get drinking water from high mountain streams."

"How are they going to get the water? Are they going to land?"

"Andy says he doesn't want to land. His strategy will be to hover, while Vik and Sluggo dip plastic pails on ropes into the stream from a trapdoor in the center of the fuselage."

"That might work. And I don't blame him for not wanting to shut down the rotors. He might not get them ignited again. And getting the water from high up in the mountains is a savvy proposition. There won't be dinosaur doo-doo in it."

"Yeah, and they won't have to boil the water. Andy got hold of purifying tablets."

"Where do you reckon he got those tablets?"

"Did I mention that I know a guy?"

Rance snorted. "What is Andy going to do for solar power, when the sun isn't shining?"

"He can skirt storms and climb above clouds. But I told him about the methane up high. It's slightly toxic, you know. And it's flammable and explosive."

"Affirmative, you warned me about that once."

"Yeah, also, Andy has batteries on board to store any surplus solar. And Vik and Sluggo will be taking turns pedaling a stationary bike. The bike is wired to generate extra electricity. Andy also installed windmill blades on the sides of the craft for additional power."

"How does Andy even know the dingus will fly?"

"He doesn't. That's why they're doing a test flight in the valley."

"Andy should stick to the steppe. I wouldn't risk flying above the rainforest."

"Yeah, Andy is going to stay close to Earth Town on the test flight. But, you know, he'll end up having to fly over jungle areas later on."

"Couldn't he just go around them?"

"Yeah, I suspect he could. And, for most of the excursion, he's going to follow the coast."

"To see if this is an island?"

"Yeah, but he also wants to survey and map the land. And he wants to catalogue the animal life, too."

"How long will that take?"

"Beats me. But they're carrying enough food for a month. They intend to be back in Earth Town by then."

"I've got to say, *amigo*: This is an awful ambitious project. Why is Andy doing it?"

"He's curious. And, you know, he's going stir-crazy in Earth Town."

"Affirmative, *amigo*. He's not one to stick in one spot very long. When Zeena died, he hightailed it out of here and headed for the Whistle Stop."

"Do you blame him?"

"Negative, I'd probably do the same."

"Yeah, me, too."

"The damsels here reckon he's a god, you know."

"Yeah, I know. And the deception will be magnified when they see him aloft."

"Andy Cooper, the flying deity."

"Yeah, more like Andy the Sky God. Or Andy in the Sky."

"A god in the sky," said Rance. "That's something you don't see every day, is it?"

"Nope, my friend, it certainly isn't."

2—ROBUR RIDES AGAIN

Craig was on hand, with his wife, Dora, when Andy and Vik (alias Victor) and Sluggo (alias David) took off on their aeronautical assessment. The aircraft resembled Robur's *Albatross*, as illustrated in the Earth Town library's copy of Jules Verne's *Robur the Conqueror.*

Earlier that day, Andy's flying machine (dubbed the *Albatross II*) had been removed from its hangar, on motorized retractable rollers—a system drafted and constructed by Roy the Mechanic, Barney the Machinist, George the Blacksmith, Bailey the Carpenter, and Craig the Electrician.

The jittery parents of Vik and Sluggo, with the rest of the Earth Town populace, watched in fascination as Andy's airship slowly and noiselessly lifted straight up. Andy, at the controls inside the wicker hull, was invisible. But Vik and Sluggo, secured by safety harnesses, were all too visible to their parents as they waved from the balcony girdling the *Albatross II.*

"It hardly makes a sound," said Roy. "We worked on that muffler system for months. But I didn't think it would function this well."

"Yeah," said Craig. "Andy wanted to run as silently as possible. He didn't want to disturb animals in their environments."

"But wouldn't the dinosaurs notice that dingus in the air?" Rance wanted to know.

"I don't think so," Craig answered. "If the textbooks are right, dinosaur eyesight isn't especially good. And they won't be looking for something in the air."

"That's providing you're right," said Rance, "about there being no flying reptiles on this planet."

"Not so loud," Craig shushed his friend. "I don't want their folks to be more anxious than they already are."

Rance grimaced. "Affirmative, *amigo*. I know how momma bears are about their cubs."

"And Linda and Nancy are definitely momma bears," the electrician quietly replied.

"Andy had me make him a compass," said Roy.

Rance was nonplused. "A compass works on this planet?"

"There seems to be a pull to the north," said Roy.

"There are established magnetic directions here?" Rance queried.

"There are," Roy replied, "if you decide that the sun rises in the east and sets in the west."

"Then," said Rance, "if you line up a compass on an east-west axis, the needle inclines northward?"

"Yep," said Roy. "It's almost like being on Earth."

A barefoot Dora, wearing mithrill shorts and her mithrill T-shirt (with the word, *Earthling*, emblazoned across the front), uttered in English: “I am seeing this. But I am not believing this.”

“And they say that seeing is believing,” Rance said to Roy.

“I can scarcely believe it myself,” Roy replied. “It’s one thing to draw up the schematics. And I knew it would work, in theory. But, to see that contraption actually leave the ground? That’s quite another matter.”

As Andy had vowed, the aircraft remained in sight of the Earth Town on-lookers for the entire shakedown cruise, which lasted for nearly an hour. When the *Albatross II* touched down at its takeoff position, with a gentle thud, the audience exhaled in relief.

“How did she handle?” Roy asked Andy, when the deity presented himself on the balcony.

“Smooth as baby oil on a billiard ball,” the god replied. “And I could see well enough out of the front and side portals.”

“How was the weight,” Roy inquired, “with all those solar panels?”

“Not bad,” said Andy. “The rotors handled it.”

“And the forward and rear propellers?” Roy asked.

“They were good, too,” Andy answered. “Better than expected. I got the velocity up to a steady ten miles per hour.”

Linda, who had been hugging her son, stalked over and gnarled: "Keep in mind that there was no wind today."

"Yes, ma'am," Andy solicitously responded.

"And there was no bad weather raging about," Linda reminded him.

"Yes, ma'am," Andy answered.

Vik made a bid to rescue his first-in-command. "Mom, we've taken all of the variables into account. And we're prepared for them."

"There's no such thing as being entirely prepared," Linda demurred.

"But we're the closest thing to it," Vik replied.

The mother fixed the god with her sternest visage. "If my child is at all harmed—"

"I won't let that happen," Andy attempted to assure her.

"Mom," said Vik, "we've got to go now."

"Everything is packed?" Linda interrogated her son.

"Checked and double-checked," replied Vik. "Really, Mom, we're taking this very seriously. One of us will always be awake and at the wheel."

"We are being diligent, Missus Collins," Sluggo chimed in. "We won't take any chances. 'Safety first.' That's our motto. We're all agreed on that."

Linda warily eyed her husband.

"They're level-headed boys," Chris said to his wife. "They'll be cautious about everything."

"And Andy knows you'll eviscerate him," said Rance, trying to inject humor, "if anything goes wrong."

"True that," said Andy.

Linda didn't crack a smile. "I don't know," she mumbled.

"They'll be okay, honey," Chris said to his wife. "We've got to let them go."

Linda opened her mouth, but she was no longer capable of discourse.

Both mothers were crying, five minutes later, when the *Albatross II* launched its inaugural voyage.

"They're heading for the *Riviera*?" Rance asked Craig.

"Yeah," the electrician answered. "They'll take a right turn at the seashore. If my hypothesis is on the noggin, it will be a circular transit."

"What if you're wrong and the *playa* stays straight? Or what if this island is a whole lot bigger than you reckon it is."

"Andy says they'll turn around when their food supplies are half gone, no matter what transpires."

"A good game-plan."

"Yeah, I'd like to think they'll stick to it."

"You don't reckon they will?"

"You know those boys," said Craig. "They might be able to talk Andy into going farther."

"Negative, *amigo*. Linda put the fear of God into the god."

"Yeah, she did, didn't she? Women keep us from getting too stupid, don't they?"

"Affirmative, *amigo*."

The denizens of Earth Town kept vigil until the *Albatross II* sunk below the curvature of the planet. They then adjourned to Hank the Baker's Quonset hut for warm biscuits and hot coffee.

Rance and Craig and Dora, however, set out for the woodland, a twelve-hour perambulation. The trio was a quarter-mile from Earth Town when Dora doffed her *Earthling* T-shirt and tossed it to her husband—as had become her costume custom.

"What does *eviscerate* mean?" Dora asked, in English.

"It's another word for *injure*," Craig answered.

"But how can a god be injured?"

"A god cannot be physically injured," Craig answered, in the woodlander tongue. "But do you recall how terrible the god felt when your chieftain died? Zeena was his best friend."

"I do recall that. You said the god would never be whole again."

"And the god would feel as bad," said Craig, "if any injury befell those boys."

"I understand," said Dora. "The mother would not have to injure the god. The god would already be injured beyond measure."

"I could not have put it better myself," said Craig.

"Affirmative," Rance rejoined, in English. "I'm glad I'm not in Andy's shoes, in more ways than one."

3—A NEW ARRIVAL

The sun had begun to set as Aleesa, with Ginger (the golden-brown, short-haired, mid-size mongrel dog) at her side, greeted the three pedestrians at the edge of the rainforest.

"Is something wrong?" the hunter asked his wife, in the woodlander tongue. "You seem distracted."

"The chieftain of the fisher folk was here today," Aleesa answered.

"That is most unusual," said Craig. "The only time I saw Paul here is when—"

"Affirmative," Rance cut him off, in English. "We don't have to go into that, *amigo*."

"Why was the fisher-folk chieftain here?" Dora asked her chieftain.

"He brought a child."

"I reckoned the shaman always brings the children," said Rance, in English.

"We are in accord, my husband," Aleesa replied, in the woodlander tongue. "But this was a special circumstance."

"What was so special about it?"

"The child was the daughter of the chieftain."

"I thought Paul had three sons by three wives," Craig said.

"His daughter was born a few days ago. She is the offspring of his newest wife."

"He brought his daughter here?" Dora asked.

Aleesa's head bobbed in answer. "The eyes of the chieftain were red. His speech was halting. I could tell he was under duress. I believe he cares deeply for this child. He left as quickly as he could. But, before doing so, he told me the name of the child is Sara."

"The big galoot has a heart," said Rance, in English.

"Don't sell him short," said Craig. "Paul might be big, but he isn't a moron. And he isn't without feelings."

"Craig," said Aleesa, "you must run to the grassland village tomorrow and tell Janis that we have need of her."

"I shall do so, My Chieftain."

As the quartet entered the rainforest, the two women fell into a private conversation—leaving the men to stroll a few paces behind them.

"I'm sorry I snapped at you back there," said Rance. "But it rankles me that the ugly bugger sees my wife as his *first wife*."

"Come on," said Craig. "You know that was a political union. Aleesa is Paul's First Wife, in name only."

"Affirmative."

"But I have to admit, it would bother me, too. I get jealous about Dora mixing with the other men in Earth Town, even if I'm at her elbow when she's doing it."

"Cupid's darts make men do batty things."

"And can you imagine what it's like for Paul? He has five wives now, if you count Aleesa."

Rance sneered. "It couldn't happen to a more deserving guy."

"It's interesting how this orphanage business developed. When we first arrived here, Zeena and her spies saved the girls who were exposed to the wild to die. Then, the shaman began bringing the babies here. And now, from what the shaman tells me, a few of the fisher folk deem it an honor for their daughters to be raised by Aleesa and her sisters."

Rance arched his brows. "Is that on the up-and-up? You aren't joshing me?"

"Nope, they know their children will have a better and easier life here, as well as being afforded the respect and attention they wouldn't receive in their own homestead. It's like those younglings won a scholarship. Nope, it's more than that. It's like they won a lottery. Like they died and went to Heaven."

"I would hardly call this Heaven, *amigo*."

"It beats a Hades of discrimination, based on melanin production."

"I'll give you that much."

"Here, at least, those girls will get a first-rate education in everything that matters. And they'll get the best medical and dental care on the planet."

"Affirmative, *amigo.* Thanks to Dan, they floss and brush after every meal."

"Yeah, Dan is a stickler for dental hygiene."

"And yet," said Rance, "these fisher-folk numbskulls continue to abandon their kids, because their skin is too light to pass the color barrier. How messed up is that?"

"I think it was Friedrich Nietzsche who said that madness, in an individual, is rare. But, in a group, it's the rule."

"I'd have to say your Friedrich friend was on the right track there. But you're preaching to the choir, *amigo.* As you know, the old ways die hard."

"Yeah, but that really isn't any excuse, is it? Stupidity, in the guise of tradition, is stupidity. No matter how you spin it."

4—THE MESSENGER

Craig set off for Earth Town before dawn. At a steady jog, he could count on making it to his destination within six hours. Today was no exception.

As Craig neared the flatland municipality in the late morn, he took note of the changes which had been made to the germinal layout of twenty slate-colored, solar-paneled Quonset huts arrayed in a circle. Amid the intervening years, a couple of paddocks had been thrown together (to hold ever-increasing herds of goats and antelope). A threshing room and flour mill and granary had been annexed for the annual cereal harvest. Concrete refrigerated block houses had been constructed (for the storage of garden and arboreal produce and milk—as well as the production of butter and cheese). Orchards of fruit and nuts (with coffee and cacao plants growing in their shade) had reached maturity. Gardens of fruits and berries and vegetables and herbs, a vineyard of table grapes, and plots of barley and rye and oats were being irrigated by pumps. A wing had been attached to the library. A garage (for the solar-powered dune buggy) and a hangar, with motorized retractable rollers (for the *Albatross II*), rounded out the scene.

Upon entering the Earth Town complex, Craig knocked on the door of Doctor Johnson's Quonset hut.

The physician welcomed him with: “Weren’t you just here yesterday? You’re becoming a frequent flyer, Mister Harrison.”

“Aleesa sent me. She came into possession of a baby girl yesterday.”

“I’ll have Roy fire up the roadster,” the physician replied. “I’m sorry there’s room for just two on it.”

“Don’t worry about me. I’ll be fine. You folks will beat me back there by a couple of hours, at the most.”

“All right. But make sure you eat something and thoroughly rehydrate before heading home. And don’t forget to restore your electrolytes.”

“I won’t forget, Doctor.”

“You know, these well-baby checkups are imperative.”

“Yeah, I know. And I appreciate your dropping everything to perform the chore.”

“Well, it’s not as though there’s any reason to stay put. No one around here gets sick. And the last instance of someone getting hurt was when Richie banged his thumb on a plumbing project.”

“You could relocate to the rainforest.”

“No thank you, Mister Harrison. I prefer an air-conditioned bungalow and clinic.”

“I don’t blame you. But it does seem like the majority of your doctoring takes place in the jungle.”

"Yes, but I'm just four hours away by dune buggy. And it's just another hour through the rainforest on foot. And we've made so many trips now that we've created a rutted road on the pampas. Roy refers to it as Highway One."

"Yeah, I like Highway One. It's a good track to run on."

"Well, it's a rather bumpy track to ride on."

"Yeah, I know. I followed the wagons towed by Vic and Sluggo. They came close to losing their loads a few times."

"I'm not surprised to hear that."

"How are Nancy and Linda holding up?"

"Not too well, I'm afraid. This is only the second time their sons have been away from home. The first was when they hauled the wicker works from the rainforest. And that was just an overnight. And the ladies knew you were looking after their sons. But, this time, the boys might be gone for as long as a month. And all they have for protection is Mister Cooper and their own good sense."

"I noticed the boys were wearing zapper holsters."

"But are zappers effective against dinosaurs? I wouldn't presume so."

Craig sucked in a breath through gritted teeth. "I should've gone in their stead."

"You know those boys would never have stood for being left behind."

"Yeah, I know. But cooler heads should've prevailed. Also, I could've talked Dora into going with us."

"Can your wife use a zapper?"

"Nope, the woodlanders don't know about zappers. They think lightning bolts shoot out of our fingertips."

"Why haven't you told them?"

"Technology like that shouldn't be spread around too freely."

"But they're going to eventually find out."

"Yeah, but we'll deal with that, when it happens. In the meantime, zappers are top-secret."

"You're probably right. But I have to ask myself: Are we protecting these people from themselves. Or are we holding them at bay? And when I say *these people*, I'm referring to the fisher folk."

"That's a good question, Doctor. An influential faction of the fisher-folk would like nothing better than to have Aleesa and her sisters leave the rainforest altogether. And never come back."

"Who told you that?"

"The shaman. He says the chieftain is managing to keep the dissidents in line. But you know how fanatics are. We narrowly averted a catastrophe at Aleesa's wedding."

"You're referring to her first wedding to the fisher-folk chieftain?"

"Yeah, by the way, the baby girl you're going to see today is the fisher-folk chieftain's daughter."

"I had a feeling something like this was going to happen someday," the physician replied. "It does seem as though there's karma at work here. What goes around, comes around. You know what I mean?"

"Yeah, I know what you mean. But the shaman tells me the fisher-folk chieftain was always against the idea of getting rid of light-skinned babies. Yet, as an office-holder, he has to play politics."

"Then, his regime is not totalitarian."

"Nope, the shaman says the fisher folk have never known omnipotent one-man rule. As I understand it, the chieftain requires the support of his council of seven elders. Without that support, the chieftain could be ousted. The fisher-folk government is closer to being a democracy than you might imagine."

"That's a good thing, right?"

"In this case, Doctor, I'm not so certain. History shows us that a strong leader, whom everyone fears and respects, can hold things together. Tito of Yugoslavia is a good model. When Tito died, the Balkans fell apart. And much suffering resulted."

"You can't seriously be against democracy."

"Nope, but, like any form of government, democracy has its limitations and drawbacks. It even went sour for the ancient Athenians. And, as you know, the Athenians practically invented democracy. The tendency of democracy is toward mediocrity."

"That sounds like a quote."

"I was paraphrasing James Fennimore Cooper."

"The man who wrote *The Last of the Mohicans*?"

"Yeah, Cooper knew about frontier folks like us."

"We really are on a frontier, aren't we?"

"Yeah, and we can only hope that we fare as well as those early Americans managed to do."

5—HOUSE CALL

A visit from Doctor Janis Johnson to Brook Haven in the Forest was consistently met with enthusiasm by young and old alike. The physician never neglected to bring sucrose-free treats with her—especially baked goods. And she habitually toted a box of Alpo biscuits (provided by Craig's covert commissary) for Ginger (the golden-brown, short-haired, mid-size mongrel dog), who was Aleesa's constant companion.

The chieftain had even granted (to the younger girls) permission to ride in the solar-powered dune buggy—with which Roy the Mechanic ferried his fiancée to and from the jungle border. The rainforest women had long ago put up a wicker garage to shelter the dune buggy, in the event of precipitation.

While Roy took the children (one by one) for brief spins on the dune buggy, Doctor Johnson saw to the medical needs of the infants, toddlers, girls, and women of the settlement—every two weeks, on average.

Although Janis was a mere five-foot-eight in height and had blond hair and pale skin, she was treated as a fellow sister by the taller and dark-haired woodland women. Every adult realized that Janis was one of the principal reasons they were leading better and longer lives than earlier generations had done.

A portion of the younger females were the offspring of men from Earth Town. But these daughters rarely visited the prairie habitations of their fathers. And they hungered for news of the grassland dwellers.

Ten of the Earth Town men had taken wives in Brook Haven in the Forest. And each had sired one child apiece.

During that same interval, eleven female infants had been brought to the women's parish by the shaman of the fisher folk. Paul's daughter, Sara, made it an even dozen.

The Earth Town fathers visited their progeny at least once a month. And they normally made the trek across the steppe in a day—staying two nights, and departing on the third day.

The men frequently brought trade items with them—customarily grain and fruits and vegetables and nuts grown in the Earth Town fields and gardens and orchards and vineyards. And they took back salted bacon, pork, and venison.

Three Earthlings were permanent tenants of Brook Haven in the Forest: Gloria Sanchez (the seamstress who also taught school and drawing and sewing and led the nightly campfire story activity) and Rance and Craig.

Although the two communities were perceptibly joined at the hip, a dozen hours of walking divided them.

Twice a year, Dan the Dentist (on the dune buggy in Roy's company) made the jaunt to do checkups and preach oral hygiene.

The one Earthling who ventured solo onto the savanna was Craig. And he sometimes did this to contact his private patron—who supplied him with odds and ends needed by the natives.

No one ever witnessed these benefactions, inasmuch as they took place in the wee hours of the morning. But everyone was grateful for the largesse.

In Earth Town dwelt three couples: Chris the Farmer and Linda, who was both the police chief and the mayor (their son was Victor/Vik), Dan the Dentist and Nancy the Nurse (their son was David/Sluggo), and Roy and Janis (who were childless). One of these couples, Dan and Nancy, was officially married. Notwithstanding, the others were linked for life.

Whenever Janis visited Brook Haven in the Forest, Sheela (the daughter of Nola and Mike the Horticulturalist) stayed by the medico's side.

It was Sheela's dream to become the in-residence physician for Brook Haven in the Forest. With this in mind, the teenager served as an apprentice to Doctor Johnson. And, since the fluently bilingual Sheela had graduated from the woodlander school, she spent many of her waking hours studying textbooks which Janis brought her.

Although Sheela was an eager and excellent student, she had given her word never to practice medicine on her own—although, on occasion, she administered first-aid to her sisters.

And Sheela knew that it would be years yet until she would be able to perform the functions of a full-fledged medical doctor—which included obstetrics, pediatrics, and gerontology.

Up to this juncture, Janis had never had to perform surgery. But Sheela was almost hoping that such an occasion might arise—even if it meant that the life of one of her sisters would be in peril.

When Sheela confessed this guilty desire to Craig, the electrician had replied: "We should always be careful what we wish for. On the other hand, ability means nothing, without opportunity. And in every tragedy and transition, there lies opportunity. And take it from me; life is all too full of tragedy and transition. The opportunity will avail itself, maybe sooner than you'd like."

6—DISQUIET

If all was tranquil between Earth Town and Brook Haven in the Forest, quite the opposite was true of the fisher-folk enclave. This was illustrated by a meeting of the seven elders in the chieftain's hut.

"We must be rid of Aleesa and her sisterhood," said the first elder, "once and for all."

"They must be driven from the rainforest," said the second elder.

"And we must build a wall," said the first elder, "to keep them out."

"You realize," said the seventh elder (named Borg), "that you are referring to your children and nieces and sisters and grandchildren and grandnieces and cousins. You got rid of them when they were infants. You put them out in the forest to die."

"Because they were imperfect," finished the third elder.

"And you are perfect?" asked Borg.

"We are more perfect than they are," answered the fourth elder.

"More perfect," Borg repeated. "That makes no sense. Do you ever listen to yourself?"

"What do you mean?" asked the fourth elder.

"You spout gibberish," said Borg, "and dare to call it wisdom."

"There is no need to be insulting," said the first elder.

"When the truth is insulting," said Borg, "it remains the truth."

"Aleesa and her sisterhood make us mine salt for them," said the second elder. "This is something they once did for themselves."

"They do not make us mine salt," Borg corrected him. "Salt is the sole commodity we can trade for bread. They do not need our fish; they fish for themselves. They do not need our milk or butter or cheese; they have goats. They do not need our vegetables; they grow their own. And they get plenty of fruit and nuts and vegetables and other commodities from the people of the grassland."

"But we like bread," said the second elder. "We want bread."

"The shaman cautioned you about bread," said Borg. "You sent your spies to Aleesa's village. And the spies told you about bread. And you said you had to have bread. And now you have bread. Yet, you complain that you must mine salt for your bread."

"Why is salt the sole commodity that Aleesa and her sisterhood desire?" asked the third elder.

"In truth," Borg retorted, "they have no need of our salt. And, if they did, they could get salt from the people of the grassland, who possess it in abundance. Aleesa and her sisterhood have no need of anything we have. They have much more than we do. They have much more than we could ever have."

"The shaman did warn you about bread," said the chieftain. "He told you that you did not need bread. Yet, you had to have bread. And now that you have bread, you complain about the cost."

"So, what if we do complain?" asked the fourth elder. "Why should Aleesa and her sisterhood have more than we do?"

"You are asking questions without meaning," said Borg. "You threw those children away. You wanted them to die, out of sight and out of mind. Instead, they prosper. Is there not a lesson here?"

"What lesson?" asked the fifth elder.

"If you have to ask that question," answered Borg, "you will never learn thc lcsson."

"We must make war on Aleesa and her sisterhood," said the sixth elder.

"If you made war on Aleesa and her sisterhood," said Borg, "you would lose that war."

"How could we lose the war?" asked the sixth elder.

"Aleesa and her sisterhood have allies," answered Borg. "And those allies have weapons beyond our ken and depth."

"We keep hearing about these weapons," said the sixth elder. "But has any one of us ever seen these weapons?"

"I have seen one of these weapons in action," replied the chieftain. "We could not stand before such weaponry."

"What of the god?" asked the fifth elder. "Would he not help us?"

"The god is angry with you," said the chieftain. "He is ashamed of you."

"Why?" asked the first elder. "What have we done to displease the god?"

"You threw away your own people," answered the chieftain. "Could there be a greater shame than that?"

"They are not our people," said the second elder. "They are imperfect."

The chieftain sighed. "I can see that my words are of no avail."

"I agree," said the third elder. "Your wisdom has failed us."

"Because you fail to be wise," said the chieftain. "One of you elders realizes this."

"Borg is too young to be an elder," objected the fourth elder.

"Borg was next in line," said the chieftain, "according to age. You know that."

"Borg is too young," said the fifth elder.

"And yet," said the chieftain, "Borg seems to be wiser than the rest of you. It is said that wisdom comes with age. But, sometimes, age arrives unaccompanied."

"We must go to war," exploded the sixth elder.

"If you make war," said the chieftain, "you will do it by yourselves."

"What do you mean?" asked the fifth elder.

"No one in the tribe," said the chieftain, "will join you in your war. It will be the six of you, against forces beyond your reckoning."

"You are mistaken," said the fourth elder. "There are others who agree with us."

"If that is true now," said the chieftain, "it will not be true on the day of your comeuppance. Or so says the shaman."

"What does the shaman mean by that?" asked the fourth elder. "What comeuppance is he talking about?"

"You will see," said the chieftain, "in the fullness of passing days."

"The god will join us in making war," the first elder blustered.

"I have told you," said the chieftain. "The god has set his countenance against you."

"How can you know this?" asked the fourth elder.

"Consider the monstrous beast," the chieftain replied. "The beast was sent by the god to protect Aleesa and her sisterhood. You fled before the beast, and rightfully so. The beast would have slain you all."

"The monstrous beast has not been seen since that day," said the fifth elder.

"The beast remains in its den," said the chieftain. "The beast is waiting for you to do something foolish, such as making war on Aleesa and her sisterhood. The beast appears when there is evil in a human heart. Thus says the shaman."

"We can defeat the beast," said the fourth elder.

"None of you can defeat the beast," said the chieftain. "I did battle with such a beast once. I know of which I speak."

"And yet," said the third elder, "we are told that the beast was once defeated."

"The beast was defeated," said the chieftain. "But not by the likes of you and me. The beast was defeated by an angel, a helper of the god, when bolts of lightning burst forth from his hands."

"We have only your word for this," said the first elder.

The chieftain looked daggers at the first elder. "Do you doubt my word?"

The first elder mutely lowered his head.

"The god will visit you," said the chieftain.

"How do you know this?" asked the second elder.

"The shaman has told me," said the chieftain.

"What will the god tell us when he visits?" asked the third elder.

"He will deliver important tidings," said the chieftain.

"Important tidings?" said the fourth elder. "What important tidings?"

“These important tidings will become apparent to you,” said the chieftain, “in the fullness of passing days.”

“What does that mean?” asked the fifth elder.

“You will see,” replied the chieftain. “Thus says the shaman.”

7—ABOVE THE SAURIANS

The sun was low in the west when Andy beheld the great salt-lake of Craig's description. The god summoned Vik and Sluggo to the foredeck of the *Albatross II* to peer out the portal with him.

The first leg of their odyssey had proceeded as Craig had advertised: A veldt of wheat-like grain, giving way to shorter grasses—and then finally to barren acreage. The valley was horseshoe-shaped—bordered by a rainforest, on the east, and two mountain ranges (with tangential foothills), on the north and south. A river flowed beside each *sierra* ridge.

Now, the voyagers were nearing the southern delta. But Andy wasn't interested in what lay beyond the tidelands.

His foremost ambition was to acquaint himself with landmass geography—and ascertain whether the valley was part of a small islet or a capacious continent. Further excursions would have to wait, since the airship cached limited provisions.

Andy had kept the *Albatross II* one hundred feet off the ground. There was no reason for going any higher, he gauged, with fair weather and slight breezes as their companions.

At a steady clip of ten miles per hour, over two cloudless days, Andy had followed the southern river and foothills and *cordillera*—dipping plastic pails into the ever-widening channel for drinking water.

The god did this mostly for the boys to hone their bucketing skills. There was already a sufficient potable-water supply aboard the vessel. Andy also wanted to try out the purification tablets, which Craig had secured from an anonymous supplier.

Throughout the dark of night, Andy held the *Albatross II* in suspension. The deity performed this hovering maneuver to simulate the nocturnal protocol he intended to follow above the *terra incognita* the aircraft would be crossing in another two days.

Andy had contemplated dropping a rope, connected to a rock, each evening. But he came to realize that such an anchor line might enable creatures to climb up and gain access to the *Albatross II.* And this would never do. Besides, an anchor would handicap the vessel with unwanted weight during the day.

It was Andy's resolution to designate landmarks at dusk, should the airship drift in the darkness. In any event, there would be a sentinel on duty to forestall any such deviation.

Andy had determined the top cruising speed of the *Albatross II* during its maiden flight by setting up mileposts. With Roy's assistance, Andy had paced off two miles on Highway One. Then, during the test run, Andy had stationed Vik and Sluggo on the balcony with a stopwatch. Sluggo signaled whenever they were directly above a milepost, while Vik monitored the chronometer. Both to and fro, the results had been the same: The aircraft covered two miles in twelve minutes.

This would serve as the measuring method on the safari: Every six minutes constituted a mile. Of course, deliberation would be given to headwinds and tailwinds and changes of direction.

But the calculations need not be exact. Andy merely wanted a general idea of the shape and size of the land below. More specific computation could be done on a future foray.

In the evenings, one person stood sentry, either in the bridge or on the balcony. And, whoever was on the balcony had to be hooked up with a safety harness. There was never a breach of this regulation.

The three adventurers also used this stoppage to take turns on the stationary bicycle, generating electricity to store in batteries.

The boys did most of the pedaling, owing to their youth and a desire to maintain their physical fitness. To that end, they also performed calisthenics and isometrics.

At the shoreline, Andy veered ninety degrees and kept to dry ground—even though this necessitated elevating the airship's altitude, as the land gradually rose up to become cliffs, while they sailed beside the strand. He didn't dare soar long above an aquatic element.

When the aircraft reached the northern river and mountain range, Andy was forced to fly over seawater—since he couldn't sufficiently escalate the *Albatross II* to surmount the peaks. Fortunately, the summits plunged into the briny depths. And Andy didn't have to go out farther than half-a-mile to get around the submerging terrain.

Prior to passing over the hydrosphere, Andy had the boys dip their buckets into the northern river, to replenish their stock—for there was no way of knowing how much potable water might lie beyond the heights.

The real estate on the far side of the crags was as arid as the topography the *Albatross II* had recently traversed. But Andy could see that, in the distance, the scrub did not extend as far inland.

No animals were evident until the aircraft crossed a short-grass expanse. Here they found grazing herbivores, which sent the boys scrambling for their sketchpads.

"We can look up what they are later," Andy said to his assistants, "and we can catalogue them then. But first, we have to capture their likenesses for our records. That's the main thing. And don't bother with coloration—at least not right away. Just jot the colors down in your notes, and you can add them to the drawings at your leisure."

The first creatures they saw were comparable to mammalian shrews.

But, as the vegetation grew higher, they glimpsed a stegosaurus.

In the forests and swamps, they found small herds of diplodocus, Apatosaurus, and brachiosaurus. These leaf-browsers were as gargantuan as any on ancient Earth, and Andy made certain to stay well away and at an elevation far beyond their craning craniums.

No one said a word until the sun was down and Andy had halted their advance. Then, the boys could no longer hold their tongues. But they spoke in hushed tones, so as not to disturb any wildlife below.

"It's like in the library books," said Vik.

"They're bigger than I thought they'd be," said Sluggo.

"They're really something," said Andy, "aren't they?"

"Do you expect there are any meat-eaters around?" Vik asked.

"I'd say those shrews might be insectivores," said Sluggo.

"Very well," said Vik. "An insectivore is technically a carnivore. But you know what I mean."

"I'm supposing the shrew species is Juramaia," said Andy, "a eutherian mammal of the Jurassic."

"Mister Harrison said he saw an Allosaurus," Sluggo submitted.

"True that," Andy replied. "We'll probably see one, too."

"I can hardly wait," said Vik.

"Let's chow down," said Sluggo. "I'm famished. I could eat anything."

"Spoken like a true omnivore," said Andy.

8—BACK AGAIN

When Craig got word from Doctor Johnson that Andy and Vik and Sluggo had landed in Earth Town, after an absence of seventeen days, the electrician bade goodbye to his spouse and legged the six hours to the colony.

Andy was coming out of the library as Craig loped into Earth Town.

The electrician greeted the sky god with: "Please tell me I didn't murder the one and only Allosaurus on this planet."

Andy guffawed. "Have no fear of that, brother. We spotted seven others."

"Were they in a group?"

"No, these were all solitary sightings."

"That's a relief, for two reasons. I told you I was afraid the Allosaurus that chased Dora might have had friends nearby. Now, I know that probably wasn't true."

"And you're right about this being an island," said Andy. "It's roughly the size and shape of Wisconsin."

"You went completely around the island?"

"Yes, we did. I estimated the perimeter to be fourteen hundred miles."

"What's that in square mileage?"

"Close to seventy thousand."

"Any volcanoes?"

"One cone. But I'm fairly sure it's extinct. It's near the center of the island. There's a lake in the caldera."

"What is the animal life like?"

"As we figured. I was just checking in the library to make sure. All of the fauna·are from the Jurassic."

"All of them?"

"Yes, every one of them. In addition to Allosaurs, we saw coelurosaurs, ceratosaurs, crocodilians, and Dilophosaurs. Those are all carnivores, you know."

"Yeah, I know."

"Plenty of herbivore specimens of brachiosaurus, diplodocus, stegosaurus, camarasaurus, and Apatosaurus. And a surprising number of mammals. Or, at least, they're suggestive of mammals. And they're much smaller than their reptilian counterparts."

"Any flying species?"

"No, except for big dragonflies. We didn't see any pterosaurs. But we did see ground-dwelling dinosaurs which bore a resemblance to birds. Those were archaeopteryx and Auromis xui. And there were small creatures gliding from tree to tree, like flying squirrels."

"How are Vik and Sluggo?"

"No worse for wear. They had a ball."

"What about you?"

"Me? I was constantly on edge. I don't want to take on that responsibility again."

"What do you mean? Might you go back?"

"At the east-southeast end of the island, I saw the tip of what might be another land mass."

"You think there's another island out there?"

"It's possible. This planet is big enough to include two islands."

"Are you going to look for this alleged isle?"

"Yes, I am. But I'm not taking Vik and Sluggo with me. I can stay out longer, if I go alone."

"You want to go by yourself?"

"I'd prefer it. Not that Vik and Sluggo weren't a big help. They were the best companions I could want. But, if I go by myself, I can stay out for three months, as opposed to one month with two deckhands aboard."

"You mean your food stores would last three months?"

"Yes, and I wouldn't have to map the place. I'd just be checking out the animal and plant life. And the geology, of course."

"How is the geology on our island?"

"The mountains of our valley are the tallest ones on the island, except for the volcanic cone."

"Any other rivers?"

"There are a few, flowing from the highlands to the sea, on all sides. So, replenishing our water supply wasn't a problem."

"How about plant life?"

"Oodles of ferns and gingkoes and cycads and conifers. Except for the desert strip on the west end, most of the island looks like a tropical paradise."

"I'm curious about something."

"What?"

"I think that desert strip keeps the dinosaurs from coming into our valley, by way of the briny deep."

"That's my hypothesis, too."

"Did you see any sea-swimming dinosaurs?"

"For the most part, we stayed away from the sea. But there were occasions when I saw big marine animals. But I didn't get close enough to identify them."

"How big were the aquatic creatures you saw?"

"About the size of orcas. But they weren't whales. I've seen whales in the ocean. And I've seen them from the air, too, on a helicopter ride. These weren't whales."

"If you go out again, you'll have to fly above salt water. Will that bother you?"

"Yes, I'd rather not do it. But I can't see any way around it. And it will give me a chance to see marine fauna better."

“I don’t envy you, my friend. Sea creatures scare the bejeebers out of me.”

“What really scares me is how Vik and Sluggo will react when they find out they’re not going with me.”

“Have you told their parents?”

“Yes, but I stopped short of telling Vik and Sluggo.”

“Crafty move. You can make the parents look like the villains.”

“It’s not that so much. And Linda, especially, seemed relieved. But, as I said, Vik and Sluggo had me constantly on edge. I came to think of them as my sons. And the burden of their presence almost became too stressful for me.”

“Does anyone else want to go with you?”

“It doesn’t matter. I’m bent on going alone.”

“Is that advisablc?”

“No, probably not.”

“Before you go, the shaman requests a favor of you.”

“The shaman? He needs a favor from me?”

“I’m expected to help you with it. Are you up for some gallivanting?”

“I’m all ears, brother.”

9—THE GOD VISITS

Twilight was gathering as dugout canoes were paddled from the wide part of the river toward the fisher-folk stronghold. The chieftain and the shaman met the approaching boats.

"Hurry in, men," the shaman urged the anglers. "Something momentous is about to occur."

As the paddlers redoubled their efforts, the shaman handed two bolls of cotton to the chieftain.

"Walk into the water," said the shaman, "until it is waist-high. Stuff these wads into your ears, so you can hear nothing. And keep your eyes on me, no matter what you may see out of the corners of your eyes. I shall signal you when you are to come ashore."

The chieftain wordlessly took the bolls, jammed them into his auditory canals, and waded outward.

A minute later, the deity, aboard the *Albatross II*, hove into view. The airship cruised slowly, thirty feet above the far side of the river. The cotton-eared chieftain was unable to hear its approach. And, true to his word, he kept his focus on the shaman.

All of the villagers had congregated by the riverside and were staring upward at the spectacle. One of them belabored the obvious by shouting: "The god is in the sky."

Andy, who was standing on the balcony of the now stationary *Albatross II*, spoke with a magnified utterance in the woodlander tongue.

“Listen to your chieftain, with whom I am well pleased. His words are my words. I speak through him. Woe to those who do not listen to their chieftain. It would be better that they had never been born.”

Some of the spectators then heard a whooshing sound. But all of them heard what followed: A loud boom overhead.

Many of the fisher folk dove to the ground or covered their heads. The remainder saw a burst of colors, streaming out in all directions, fifty feet above the *Albatross II*.

This concussion was followed by two more blasts—and two more colorful displays—higher than the first.

When the villagers finally collected their wits, the deity and his aircraft were gone.

The shaman beckoned to the chieftain, who worked his way toward the beach.

“You all saw the god,” said the shaman to his tribe, in the loudest colloquy he could muster. “You all heard his words. Never forget this day. And never forget his message. The god will not be seen again.”

“What happened?” inquired the chieftain, once he had removed the cotton from his ears.

The shaman patted the eight-foot-tall chieftain on his titanic chest. “Your troubles with the elders are over.”

The chieftain's brows furrowed. "For how long?"

"Long enough," the shaman replied. "The rest will take care of itself."

The chieftain nodded toward the boggled mob. "What ails them?"

"They recently had a visit from the god."

"They did?" asked the addled chieftain. "I saw nothing. I heard nothing."

"And people will not forget this."

"I do not understand. Why did the god visit?"

"The god came here to deliver a ringing endorsement."

"I have no idea what you just said."

"Be not concerned, My Chieftain. Walk toward your people. Smile at them. You are now a giant among them."

"But I have been a giant for many cycles of the stars."

"Not like you are today."

The chieftain grunted. "I do not know what you mean."

"It matters not."

"I am not a wise man."

"You are wiser than you believe yourself to be, Paul. Now, go to your people. They have need of your assurances."

The chieftain grunted again.

"And, Paul," the shaman appended, "be especially nice to the elders. That will disturb them greatly."

"I am glad you are on my side," said the chieftain. "But I am, at the moment, not quite sure why."

The shaman laughed lightly. "This is as it ought to be," he replied.

10—BACK TO EARTH TOWN

"I followed the script," said Andy, "word for word. I went *Old Testament* and *New Testament* on them. Did it do any good?"

"From all accounts," Craig answered, "you were stupendous. The fireworks were a nice touch. Where did you get them?"

"Vik and Sluggo made them," said the deity. "They've been working on them in their spare time. And they were spoiling for a chance to try them out."

"I'm impressed," said Craig. "And I imagine all of the fisher folk were, too. I suspect one of the boys was behind the wheel."

"Yes, Vik was at the helm. And Sluggo shot off the pyrotechnics from the blind side of the *Albatross II*."

"Please thank the boys for me. Where are they, by the way?"

"They went fishing. They won't be back for a few days."

"Have you told them, yet?"

"No."

"You're not planning to take off while they're away, are you?"

"No, that would be craven. I'll wait until their return."

"And you said their parents know they're not going with you?"

"Yes, and they're ecstatic."

"At least you'll have four people in your corner."

"Yes, that's something, at least."

"I wish you weren't going by yourself, my friend."

"It's better this way."

"But is it? Too many things can go wrong. Even if you chewed Dora's special leaves, you couldn't stay awake for more than two or three days straight."

"True that, brother. But I really can't ask anyone else to come with me."

"Yeah, I know. Everyone around here has children or spouses or other responsibilities."

"Thanks again for the microphone and the loudspeaker. Where did you get that equipment?"

Craig winked. "I know a guy."

"You keep telling me that."

"Well, you keep asking."

"It's not that I'm griping, brother. You did give me the cacao plants I wanted. And Chris and Mike brought in the first cocoa crop, just three years later."

"Bless their hearts. It turns out that we have the perfect conditions here for growing *Theobroma cacao*."

"*Theobroma* means 'Food of the Gods' in Greek, you know."

"Well named."

"And Hank blended a fine milk chocolate."

"Bless Hank, too."

"Perchance you can ask 'the guy you know' whether he knows a traveling companion for me."

"I'll see what I can do. But I thought you wanted to fly solo."

"I'm having second thoughts."

"Yeah, second thoughts are okay. They beat no thoughts at all."

"Vik and Sluggo told me you got them a telescope for stargazing. And it's a top-of-the-line model."

"Yeah, it's okay. I knew they wouldn't need anything fancy, though. It's not like they can use a computerized one, since the sky is entirely different here."

"Vik and Sluggo said they found wanderers."

"Wanderers? As in planets?"

"You bet. They found a big planet with at least four moons."

"You mean, like Jupiter?"

"Yes, but, of course, it couldn't be Jupiter. But it looks like Jupiter. And they found something else, too."

"What?"

"Five celestial objects that don't move."

"What do you mean: They don't move?"

"They seem to be satellites in geosynchronous orbits."

"What makes the boys think they're satellites?"

"The objects reflect sunlight, like a planet or a moon. But they don't emit any light, in and of themselves."

"That's curious."

"Yes, I agree. And there's something else. The objects are in a line. And they're evenly spaced."

"In an arc?"

"Yes, they go from west-northwest to east-southeast. And one of them is directly overhead."

"Do you have a hypothesis?"

"Not a clue."

"We have a mystery then."

"And that calls to mind another Jules Verne novel: *Mysterious Island*."

"Yeah," Craig replied. "*Mysterious Island* is an appropriate title. For this place is, without doubt, an isle of mysteries."

11—BAKA

"Master," said the shaman's apprentice, "the elders asked me to make Baka for them."

"I presume you told them that you are prohibited from making Baka," replied the shaman.

"I did tell them, Master. I told them Baka is forbidden to make. And I told them it is forbidden to eat."

"Loda, do you know why the elders want Baka?"

"I can venture a guess, Master."

"What would be your guess, Loda?"

"The elders believe that eating Baka will make them impervious to harm."

"Ah, the old lie."

"Are you sure this is a lie, Master?"

"Truly, it is a lie, Loda. But many fools, down through the ages, have believed otherwise."

The apprentice pursed his lips and looked troubled.

"Be not dismayed," said the shaman. "I shall give you permission to make Baka for them."

"But, Master, I do not know how to make Baka."

"Be not dismayed, Loda. I shall give you the ingredients and show you how to make Baka."

"But, Master, it is forbidden to make Baka."

"And with good reason, Loda. This is why I shall not give you the key ingredient."

"Then, Master, it will not truly be Baka."

"It will not truly be Baka, Loda."

"And I shall not be committing a forbidden act."

"You will not be committing a forbidden act," the shaman verified.

"Will the false Baka be safe to eat, Master?"

"It will be entirely safe to eat, Loda. This is not to say that the false Baka might not make the elders act foolishly. But the elders are accustomed to acting foolishly."

"Then I shall be doing no harm, Master?"

"You will be doing no harm, Loda."

"What makes you think the elders will again ask me to make Baka?"

"The elders are a predictable and persistent bunch, Loda. They will keep pestering you, until you make Baka for them."

"Why would the elders want to be impervious to harm?"

"The elders fear the monstrous beast on the pathway, Loda. And they fear the weaponry of Aleesa and her sisterhood."

"Do you believe the elders intend to kill the beast and attack the home of Aleesa and her sisterhood?"

"As I said, Loda, the elders are a persistent and predictable bunch."

The apprentice frowned. "I see, Master."

"Tell me, Loda. How many of the elders approached you?"

"Six of them approached me, Master."

"Borg was not among them?"

"Borg was not among them, Master."

"This is encouraging, Loda. I believe Borg to be a good man."

"What if the elders act under the influence of the Baka, Master? Will they not be endangered then?"

"Be not dismayed, Loda. The elders will never be endangered."

"Then, Master, what will happen to the elders?"

"Wait, Loda, and you will see in the fullness of passing days. It will be a wondrous thing to behold."

12—THE BAKA EATERS

Loda was asleep, a few days later, in the wee hours of the morning, when the six eldest elders entered his hut. The first elder seized Loda by the shoulders to awaken him.

"What is it?" the groggy shaman's apprentice inquired.

"You have a fine family, Loda," the first elder said. "A mother and two sisters and a brother, alive and well."

Loda was no longer groggy.

"It would be a shame if something bad happened to them," said the second elder.

"What do you mean?" was the apprentice's timorous rejoinder.

"We want you to make Baka for us," said the third elder.

"I am prohibited from making Baka. You know this."

"We do not care that you are prohibited," said the fourth elder.

"Let me be clear about this, Loda," said the first elder. "If you want to see that no harm comes to your family, you will make Baka for us."

A wide-eyed Loda queried: "Are you saying you will harm my family, if I do not make Baka for you?"

“Truly,” said the second elder, “you take our meaning.”

“Do you know how to make Baka?” asked the third elder.

“I know how Baka can be made.”

“If it is forbidden to make Baka,” delved the fourth elder, “how is it that you know how to make Baka?”

“I am not forbidden to know how to make Baka. There is a difference between knowing and doing.”

“You are sharp of wit,” said the fifth elder, “for so early in the day.”

“Make Baka now, Loda,” demanded the first elder.

“It will take me a while to gather the ingredients and prepare the mixture,” Loda temporized.

“How long will that take?” asked the fifth elder.

“If I go out at first light to gather the ingredients, I can have the finished product by nightfall.”

“You have one day, Loda,” said the first elder. “We shall visit you tomorrow, here, at this same time.”

“Keep in mind how dear your family is to you, Loda,” said the second elder.

With that, the six elders slunk out of Loda’s lodgings.

Instead of going back to sleep, the shaken apprentice crept through the moonlit darkness to the shaman’s hut. But Loda was careful to proceed indirectly, lest he be followed. He moved from abode to abode, stopping to look about him and listening for footsteps. Finally, when he was convinced that no one was hot on his zigzag trail, he approached the shaman's domicile.

"Come in, Loda," said the shaman, before the apprentice could divulge his presence.

"How did you know it was I, Master?"

"I am surprised that you would need to ask, Loda, after all the cycles of the stars we have spent in each other's company."

The apprentice entered and sat opposite from the cross-legged shaman.

"They threatened my family, Master. The elders—"

"Say no more," the shaman interrupted. "I know everything. The elders want you to make Baka for them to eat. And they made you an offer you could not refuse."

"Master, I—"

"Be not dismayed, Loda. I shall bring Baka to your hut tomorrow night. And we shall wait for the elders together."

"I do not think they expect you to be there, Master."

"Be not dismayed, Loda. They will not see me."

"Master, my family—"

"Be not dismayed, Loda. Your family is safe, and will remain safe. Go home and get some sleep. At sunrise, go into the rainforest and pretend to gather Baka ingredients. It matters not what you gather, Loda. Even if the elders are watching you, they know nothing about making Baka. And, if they memorize what you gather, it will do them no good."

"I see, Master."

"I thought you would, Loda."

"I am truly ashamed, Master."

"Be not ashamed, Loda. You have done nothing wrong. In fact, you have done well by coming to me so swiftly."

The apprentice managed a sickly smile and left the shaman's quarters.

"I must trust that my master knows what he is doing," Loda said to the darkness, "because I have no idea what I am doing."

*****

At sunrise, as he had been directed, Loda went into the jungle and made a show of searching for plants on the ground, pulling up random roots, and plucking various blossoms and inedible berries from trees and bushes.

That evening, when Loda entered his lodgment, he was relieved to find half-a-dozen packets lying on the ground by his pallet.

The subsequent morning, the apprentice was awake, awaiting the elders.

The elders entered, on schedule, and found Loda sitting on his pallet. In front of the apprentice lay the six packets.

"Are these presents for us?" asked the first elder.

"Is my family safe?" the apprentice inquired.

"Be not dismayed, Loda," said the second elder. "Your family is safe."

"Then," said Loda, "these presents are for you."

"Where is the shaman?" asked the third elder. "We have not seen him all day."

"I have not seen him, either. But then, I have been busy."

"Be not dismayed, Loda," said the fourth elder. "You have done the right thing."

"You are serving the best interests of the tribe," said the fifth elder.

"The tribe," the other elders echoed.

"We know what is best for the tribe," the first elder said.

"The tribe," the other elders echoed.

"Go ahead," said Loda. "Take your presents. They are what you wanted. Take them, and leave me and my family in peace."

"First," said the sixth elder, "we want you to eat a small portion from all six of our presents."

"You do not trust me?"

"It is not that we do not trust you," said the sixth elder.

"It is that we do not trust the shaman," said the fifth elder.

"Truly," said the fourth elder, "you are too simple a man to fool us, Loda."

"You want me to eat a bit of each of your presents?" Loda sought confirmation.

"If you would be so kind," purred the first elder.

"Indulge us," the second elder harshly recommended.

Loda's heart was in his throat, but he resolutely did as he was bidden.

"Now," said the first elder, "we shall wait to see how the Baka affects you."

Silence reigned for a long minute.

Then, the second elder spoke up: "You are perspiring, Loda."

"Truly, I am perspiring," said the apprentice, wiping his forehead. "I must admit to being upset by all that has recently occurred."

"You do not feel ill, Loda?" asked the third elder.

"Truly, I do feel a little ill. But then, I have not eaten anything all day. And my family has been threatened. That would make anyone feel ill."

"We would not have harmed your family," said the fourth elder. "It was an empty threat."

"How was I to know this?"

"That is correct, Loda," said the fifth elder. "You had no way of knowing."

"As you can see, Loda," said the sixth elder, "we are clever men. We are too clever for the likes of you."

The apprentice winced. "Truly, I am not a clever man."

"You are blinking, Loda," said the first elder. "Do your eyelids grow heavy?"

"I have not slept since your last visit."

"Perhaps you should lie back and get some rest now, Loda," said the second elder. "We shall remain here, to be sure that you do not become more ill."

"If you do not mind, I shall remain awake until you leave."

"You fear us, Loda?" asked the third elder.

"Any sane man would fear the likes of you; much less go to sleep in your presence."

"You are becoming cheeky," said the fourth elder.

"I am feeling braver."

"Boldness is one of the effects of the Baka," related the fifth elder.

The apprentice yawned. "I have changed my mind," he said. "I can hardly keep my eyes open. I shall rest now. You gentlemen can find your way out, I trust."

Loda reclined on his pallet and closed his eyes. Within moments, his breathing was shallow and regular.

"He is asleep," said the sixth elder, drawing a knife. "Shall we see if the Baka has taken effect?"

"Put your blade away," barked the first elder. "Baka does not work that fast. Loda is not yet impervious to harm. Baka takes much longer to be fully effective. But when it does take effect, one is impervious for long afterward."

"How do you know this?" asked the sixth elder.

"My father's father told me," answered the first elder, "when I was very young."

"How did your father's father know?" asked the sixth elder.

"His father's father told him," the first elder replied, with growing irritation. "Enough with the questions."

"Let us take our presents and hasten to my home," said the second elder. "All of our weapons are stashed there. We can eat the Baka and go to sleep and awaken and slay the monster and go to war against Aleesa and her sisterhood."

"It is in the best interests of the tribe," said the third elder.

"The tribe," the other elders echoed.

The six extortionists stole away into the semi-darkness. When they arrived at the hut of the second elder, they entered and sat upon the ground, and greedily devoured the contents of the packets.

Five minutes therewith, they were all asleep.

This is when the shaman commenced his work.

13—CHANGED MEN

Loda emerged from his hut, as the sun was rising, and trudged to the river to slake his thirst. The fishermen had not yet taken to their canoes, so the apprentice had the waterfront to himself for a few minutes.

Loda brooded over the events of the past two days and was curious as to why the shaman hadn't put in an appearance.

"Could my master have forgotten?" Loda asked no one in particular.

"I did not forget," he heard, in reply.

The apprentice whirled about to see his master standing behind him.

"Let us take a walk," said the shaman. "You must have questions. And the answers to these questions should not be overheard by others."

"We shall walk then," replied the apprentice. "Lead the way, please, Master."

Both men were quiet until they came to a sand bar.

"Loda," the shaman said, "you were courageous last night."

"I did not feel courageous, Master."

"Even so, Loda, you were courageous. And because of your bravery, all is now well."

"How is it well, Master?"

"I think you will find the six elders, the ones who accosted you, to be changed men."

"How is this so, Master?"

"I accompanied the elders to their lair last night."

"What transpired there, Master?"

"The elders consumed the contents of their packets and fell asleep. And then I spoke to them."

"What did you say, Master?"

"I told the elders that they must be good people from now on."

"Did the elders hear you in their sleep, Master?"

"The elders heard me, because they had eaten hypnotic seeds."

"You have not told me about such seeds, Master."

"There was no need, Loda, until now."

"But now you will tell me?"

"Now I shall tell you, Loda. There are seeds on a rare plant, which grows half-a-day's walk from here, on the opposite side of the river. Eating the seeds of this plant will bend the minds of men and women to another's will."

"These are powerful seeds, Master."

"Truly, they are powerful seeds, Loda. And not seeds to be misused."

"I shall always keep this in mind, Master."

"Tell me, Loda, how did you sleep last night?"

"I must have slept deeply, Master, for I awoke refreshed."

"Do you feel any different?"

"I feel much relieved, Master, now that you have told me that all is well."

"Loda, I am going to say a few words. They are words you have never heard. And they will not make sense to you. Are you ready?"

"I am ready, Master."

"Franz Friedrich Anton Mesmer."

The apprentice clapped his hands twice, turned in a full circle, and sat.

"Master," yelped the frightened apprentice, as he sprang to his feet, "what just happened?"

"Be not dismayed, Loda. Last night, I told you to sleep deeply. Then, I told you to do what you have just done, when I said certain words. The words you just heard."

"Then, Master, the words did not make me do these things."

"I made you do these things, Loda. I, and the power of the seeds."

"These are truly powerful seeds, Master."

"And may I say once again, Loda, they are not seeds to be misused."

"I shall always keep this in mind, Master."

"Someday, Loda, I will show you the plant of which I spoke and demonstrate how the seeds of it can be used. But for now and always, this will be our secret."

"Some secret, Master."

"It is truly some secret, Loda."

"Master, what will become of the six elders?"

"From now on, the six elders will act pleasantly, especially to you. They will not know why they are being pleasant. But you will know, Loda. And you must never tell them, or anyone else, what you know."

"It is a secret, Master?"

"Truly, it is a secret, Loda. Furthermore, the six elders will agree with their chieftain and will never act disagreeably toward any other person."

"Will the elders know that they have changed, Master?"

"They will not be aware of the change, Loda. Everyone else will notice, of course. But everyone else will likely not say anything about it to the elders."

"Why is that, Master?"

"It is the way people are, Loda. They will talk among themselves. But then, after manifold fillings of the moons, no one will recollect how disagreeable the elders once were."

"And the elders, Master. Will they have no memory of what they have been doing lately?"

"Truly, Loda, they will have no memory of it."

"But, Master, I want the elders to keep their memories. I want them to be ashamed that they threatened my family. I want them to feel shame for their cruelty toward me."

"You seek revenge, Loda?"

"Truly, Master, I seek revenge."

"In a sense, Loda, you will have your revenge."

"I do not see how, Master."

"You will see, Loda, in the fullness of passing days."

"I am not a patient man, Master."

"You will learn patience. And you will learn the folly of holding a grudge. Holding a grudge, Loda, is like eating poisonous berries, and hoping your enemy will die from your doing so."

"But it is not easy to let go of grudges, Master."

"If letting go of grudges was easy, Loda, everyone would do it."

"I still have much to learn, do I not, Master?"

"Truly, you have much to learn. And you have much growing to do. But the learning and growing must be done, Loda, for you to become a shaman."

"It is not until this moment, Master, that I came to realize how different and special a shaman must be."

"Truly, Loda, a shaman must be different from all men and women. But he cannot think himself so special that he becomes proud. Pride is a trap, Loda. It is a lovely lure that deceives and destroys. You and I must be above pride. We ought to have pride in our work, of course. But we must walk and act with humility. And we must remain humble. For whenever we feel proud of our humility, we shall have lost it. Humility is like smoke. It dissipates with the slightest breeze."

"I believe I know your meaning, Master."

"Being a shaman, Loda, is a difficult road to travel."

"But a worthwhile road to travel, Master, is it not so?"

"It is truly a worthwhile road to travel, Loda. More worthwhile than you might yet realize."

14—KOREE STEPS UP

"Gloria wants to palaver," said Dora to Craig, in English.

Dora's spouse smirked. "You've been hanging out with Rance a lot, haven't you?"

"Did I say something wrong?"

"Nope, in fact, it was cute."

"I am pleased then," Dora said, with a grin. "Gloria wants to see us after school today."

Craig glanced upward. "It's almost noon now. School must be letting out."

"Let us go then, my husband."

The couple crossed the compound to a thatched open-air pavilion, which had been built for Craig when he became the district's first schoolteacher—a position which currently belonged to Gloria.

"Dora tells me you have something on your mind," Craig said to Gloria.

The schoolmistress, who was collecting papers from desks, replied: "Good timing, you two. The school day just ended."

"What's up?" Craig asked.

"You know Koree," said Gloria.

"Yeah, she was one of my students."

"And you hired her to climb a tree once."

"Yeah, I did."

"You know that Koree is strong and agile and quick-witted."

"Yeah, I do."

"Koree is also the best artist here."

"Yeah, I know. I've seen her illustrations at the campfire story time."

"Koree isn't a teenager anymore."

"Yeah, granted."

"She helps me with the kids."

"Good for her," said Craig, "and good for you."

"But I can spare Koree for a while."

"Spare Koree? Spare her for what?"

"You know what Koree saw on the day she climbed the tree for you."

Craig blanched. "Koree said she would keep that a secret."

"And she did keep it a secret. But word gets around."

"Rance's Rangers blabbed?"

"Men tend to talk."

"Yeah, they do."

"Well, since then, Koree has wanted to overcome her fear."

"Fear? What fear?"

"Fear of what she saw that day. She still has nightmares."

"That's too bad. And I'm sorry about that. But how can I be of assistance?"

"Koree wants to go with Andy."

"You mean Koree wants to ride in the *Albatross II*?"

"More than that. She wants to go with Andy on his flight of exploration."

"Oh, I see. Ah, but, uh, well, would that be appropriate?"

"I don't see why it wouldn't."

"But, ah, um, well, you know, a young woman alone with an older man. There might be, you know, certain problems."

"Such as?"

"Well, uh, just for starters—"

"Is Andy worried about what other people might say?"

"I, uh, I'm not certain. I know that sounds silly, in our situation and all. But, well, you know how people can be."

"Are you saying Koree can't go because she's a female?"

"Well, ah—"

Gloria glared. "Are you really going there, Craig?"

"Uh, well, it's more that Andy worries about the safety of his crewmembers. You can understand that."

"Koree is sharp enough to stay safe. She has climbed hundreds of trees and gone on hundreds of hunts. And she has never been injured."

"My chieftain is all for it," Dora broke in.

Craig was stunned. "Aleesa signed off on this?"

"Sure," said Gloria. "Why not?"

"Well, ah, um, I'm at a loss for words."

"You'll arrange everything then?"

"Ah, well, uh, I'll see what I can do."

"That's good enough for me. I'll tell Koree."

"But—"

"If anyone can make this happen, you can, Craig."

"But—"

"If you'll excuse me now, I told a few of the girls I'd go on a hunt with them this afternoon."

"Ah, yeah, good hunting."

As Gloria strode off, Craig addressed Dora. "You knew about this?"

"I knew what Gloria was going to ask you."

"And you believe this to be a good idea?"

"Koree wants an adventure. I'm all for adventure. You know that."

“Yeah, I know, but—”

“So, it’s a done deal?”

“You have been hanging around Rance a lot, haven’t you?”

“Rance believes it’s a good idea.”

“Am I the last to learn about this?”

“Well, I don’t know everyone.”

“Funny lady.”

“The god does not know, yet.”

“He will soon find out about it, though.” Craig scratched his head. “And I guess he’ll find out about it from me.”

“You will be leaving now, my husband?”

“You want me to run to Earth Town now?”

“I told the girls I’d join them on their hunt.”

“Then, I have my marching orders, apparently.”

Dora tapped a forefinger against her cheek.

Craig kissed her where she had indicated.

“Happy hunting,” he said.

“Good luck with the god,” answered Dora. “And come back safely.”

15—ANDY IS AMENABLE

Craig had six hours of jogging to come up with a good argument for Andy's taking on Koree as a passenger. Since the electrician wasn't sold on the idea—how, he asked himself, was he going to get the deity to go along with it?

Craig did, however, feel guilty that Koree had suffered bad dreams after seeing an Allosaurus—even if it wasn't the real McCoy, but a three-dimensional mockup, virtually concocted at the last minute by two fellows from Bedford, England, who televised the actions of the Earthlings in the valley.

These two fellows were "the guy" Craig knew: His contact for any item someone in Earth Town or Brook Haven in the Forest required.

Principally, Craig dealt with Reginald Wylie nowadays. Reginald's partner, Creighton Beryl, ostensibly had better things to do than to act as Craig's personal gofer.

But then, Reginald knew where everything was stored—and where everything that wasn't stored could be procured. Creighton had continually depended on Reginald in such matters.

The electrician never inquired as to where Reginald acquired the items Craig requested. And Reginald never offered any explanations. It was a convenient arrangement.

Craig could follow the logic in Koree's supposition that seeing monsters from a vaulted vantage might cure her of nightmares.

"It's worth a try," he propounded.

And, as Dora had argued: "Koree wants an adventure."

*****

When Craig conversed with Andy in the Earth Town library, the god didn't need much convincing. Andy had known Koree, since she was a little girl, and recognized that Koree would serve as an admirable assistant.

"I have more packing to do," Andy said to Craig, "mostly to stock dried food. And there are a few last-minute details I must attend to."

"What shall I say to Koree?"

"Please ask that estimable young woman to wait for me by the medical facility at the edge of the rainforest. I'll be dropping by in two days, aboard the *Albatross II*, probably around noon."

"Koree isn't a big eater. In fact, she mostly munches on those special leaves Dora favors."

"I'm not so much concerned about our food supply as I am about privacy issues. The boys and I didn't have them."

"Yeah, I thought about that, too. But maybe you two can work out a system."

"Yes, we probably can. We're both reasonable people. And I'll furnish all of the art materials Koree will need for sketching."

"I'll tell Koree."

Andy held up a hand. "But I'm not going to give Koree a zapper. She'll have to provide her own weapons."

"I don't think that will be a problem. Koree is almost as good with a spear as Dora is. And she learned her archery skills from Gloria."

"Is that pint-sized seamstress still running things in the women's burg?"

"Yeah, pretty much. Gloria teaches school and sewing and drawing. And she coordinates the campfire story each night. And she's the best archer in the borough."

"And I once supposed that Gloria would be too fragile for rainforest living. I sure got that wrong."

"Gloria surprised a lot of people. She even surprised herself. She told me so."

"I can't say for sure how long this flight will take. But Koree and I should have enough food for sixty days."

"I suspect, if you had to, you could live off the land."

"Yes, we probably could. But I don't want it to come to that."

"Yeah, I'd feel the same way."

"My aim is to go out to the horseshoe's end and bear east-southeast, until we locate land. The main goal will be to find and catalogue the flora and fauna, if there is any."

"Why not just fly over the mountains directly south of rainforest border? It would be a shorter route."

"Yes, it would be shorter. But the *Albatross II* can't ascend high enough to clear any of those summits."

"How high can it go?"

"I haven't tried, yet. But I'm supposing three hundred feet is its limit. At least, that's what the math and physics tell me."

"You'll have to do some training with Koree. She'll need education in the fine arts of pedaling a stationary bicycle and dipping plastic pails into mountain streams."

"She'll do fine. As for being up in the air, Koree has no trouble climbing the tallest trees."

"Yeah, I had the same thought."

"Since you'll have the opportunity to tell Koree how the *Albatross II* flies and functions, we might as well go over to the ship and I'll show you what little you don't already know."

"You're certain you're okay with this?"

"As certain as I am of anything on this planet," Andy answered, "which, if I'm to be completely honest, is not very certain at all."

16—KOREE LEAVES THE NEST

Two days later, as arranged, Koree was waiting by the woodland medical facility at noon. But Koree wasn't alone. The entire sorority was on hand to see her off.

When the *Albatross II* became conspicuous in the western sky, there was much excitement among the females. Many of them had worked on the wicker for the vessel's fuselage. But they had no idea what the completed structure would look like. And it approximated nothing in their experience or imagination. The sisterhood would come to call it "the Floating Hut."

The airship landed with a gentle thud, and Andy stepped onto the balcony. Ginger (the golden-brown, short-haired, mid-size mongrel dog) whined at seeing her erstwhile owner. Andy heard the sound, saw Ginger, and waved. But the canine didn't stir from Aleesa's side.

Koree picked up her spear and bow and quiver and drinking receptacle, and stepped through the balcony door, which Andy had opened for her. The deity fastened Koree with a safety harness and retired to the fuselage.

While the *Albatross II* slowly ascended, Koree's eyes welled with tears as she bade farewell to the only family she had known. This would be her first extended time away from them. And she already felt pangs of homesickness.

But there was no trepidation in Koree's heart. She knew she was doing the right thing. This voyage was not simply something she wanted to undertake. It was something she felt she had to do.

When Koree could no longer see her sisters at the rainforest's edge, she entered the fuselage. Andy greeted her on the bridge, in the woodlander tongue, and asked her if she wanted to take the wheel. He didn't have to make the offer twice.

Craig had told Koree about the *Albatross II* and how it worked, so she already knew the basics. She listened intently to everything the god told her, as they set a diagonal course for the river on the south side of the valley.

Koree was always careful to rig up her safety harness, whenever she left the fuselage of the aircraft. Although the *Albatross II* was a scant forty feet in the air, Koree knew a fall from such a height could be fatal—and most likely debilitating.

Koree practiced scooping up water from the southern stream, until she was proficient with the maneuver. Although the young woman would be able to safely drink river water, without it being sanitized, she knew it was essential (for Andy's sake) to pop in a purification tablet, and let the plastic pail sit for a few minutes, before she poured the contents into the storage tank.

The stationary bicycle took some getting used to, though. Koree was deft at running and jumping. And her sense of balance, from climbing trees, was keen. But there was nothing in her past which prepared her for moving her legs in a cycling motion. For all that, by their third day out, Koree was able to pedal non-stop for an hour.

In the nighttime, Koree and Andy stood watch in four-hour shifts. Koree didn't need as much sleep as Andy did, insomuch as she chewed Dora's special leaves. But she slept four full hours, all the same.

Craig had also familiarized Koree with the immense body of water awaiting them. But being informed is one thing; seeing is quite another. And Koree was spellbound at the literal vision of this geographical feature.

Once they reached the other side of the mountains, Andy kept the *Albatross II* one hundred feet aloft, as he had done on his previous flight. But, even at such an altitude, Koree was easily able to make out the shapes and sizes of the animals below.

Koree's initial encounter with an Allosaurus was spine-tingling. Even though Andy had avowed that the saurian's sense of sight was poor, Koree was convinced that the therapod's gaze had followed their every movement.

Andy had also claimed that the jaws of the Allosaurus were, at the most, twelve feet from the ground. But Koree didn't think eighty-eight feet of clearance was sufficient for the *Albatross II*. And she had an arrow in her drawn bow, all the while the Allosaurus was within range.

Koree's apprehension rose to its zenith when she and Andy glided above an Apatosaurus herd. The heads of these herbivores were capable of reaching twenty-five feet into the air. Although this afforded the *Albatross II* a safety margin of seventy-five feet, Koree nonetheless found these fifty-thousand-pound creatures to be daunting.

At daybreak, over an east-southeast location, Andy banked the *Albatross II* inland and traced a rivulet to its highland source. There, Koree retrieved enough freshwater to fill the storage tank—for the airship was about to embark upon its seaward sojourn.

The horizon in that direction was filled with clouds. But Andy, trusting that his records were reliable, steered his aircraft according to the logged compass reading.

At a speed of ten miles per hour and an altitude of one hundred feet, Koree descried land, through a break in the clouds, five hours after leaving their home turf.

At intervals, she and Andy could make out dark shapes in the placid water below them. But they didn't see a single marine organism break the saline surface. For this, both aeronauts were grateful.

Within seven hours, the *Albatross II* was flying above lush vegetation which teemed with fauna. Among the mosses, ferns, and conifers crept small mammals—and what appeared to be hummingbirds and crow-like reptiles, which flitted between tree branches.

Koree dashed off drawings, right and left, of different dinosaur species—none of which, Andy noted, resided on the cay they'd left behind them. This region seemed to be home to a different age of Earth's history. The strangest creature looked to be a blend of a pig and a cow and a turtle.

One biped was physically similar to an Allosaurus. But it was patently a plant-eater. And it was recurrently found in herds.

Another animal gave every indication of being a colossal crocodile, to Andy's way of thinking. And this brute offered up ample evidence, by feeding on a carcass, that it was not an herbivore.

Koree and Andy also saw heavily armored quadrupeds and lumbering lizards with rounded fins on their backs.

After days of soaring and sketching, Andy notified Koree that they were heading homeward.

The young woman pointed in an east-southeast direction and said, in the woodlander tongue: "But there is more land that way."

"You have good eyes," said Andy. "I did not see anything."

"It is there," Koree replied.

"You're sure?" Andy asked, in English.

"I'm sure," she answered.

Andy entered the compass reading into the ship's log.

"Well, then," the deity responded, in the woodlander tongue, "we shall have to look into that someday. But, for now, I must get you back to your loved ones. They will be missing you. And you will have much to tell them."

17—TRIASSIC WORLD

"The animals were all from the Triassic," Andy reported to Craig. "And the plants were Triassic, too."

"The Triassic, huh? That's interesting."

"I looked them up in the library when we got back." Andy held up a list in his notebook. "Koree's sketches were of rhynchosaurs, staurichosaurs, phytosaurs, listrosaurs, aetosaurs, rauisuchians, proterosuchus, coelophysis, plateosaurs, postosuchus, tanystropheus, and cynodonts. All of the reptiles were archosaurs: The forerunners of Jurassic dinosaurs."

"And Koree's representations are authentic?"

"Right on the money. She's an excellent artist."

"How did Koree fare, by the way?"

"She was fine. A real trouper. I couldn't have done it without her."

"Koree never got scared?"

"I won't say that. But she was no more frightened than I was. Some of those varmints are the stuff of nightmares."

"Speaking of which, do you suspect Koree will continue to have nightmares of Allosaurs."

"If this flight didn't cure her, brother, I doubt that anything else could. We were in the midst of the most dangerous-looking critters you can find."

"And it was an island, like this one?"

"Yes, it was an island. And it was like our island. Not quite as big, though. But the shape was much the same."

"And you say there's more land to the east?"

"Koree says so. And I trust her eyesight and judgment."

"You're going out there again?"

"Sure. What's the worst that could happen? We'd find out that Koree was wrong. Or perchance we'll find another island."

"But what kind of world would it be?"

"Yes, that's the question, isn't it?"

"Verily, my friend. But would Koree be willing to go again?"

"I doubt that I could stop her, brother."

"How did Vik and Sluggo handle not going with you?"

"I know they were displeased. But they did their best not to show it, especially in front of their parents."

"The boys had an escapade of their own, while you were gone."

"What escapade was that?"

"They visited the woodland women."

Andy was askance. “Why would they do that? The women’s burg is an all-day tramp from Earth Town.”

“They got permission from their parents, and from Aleesa, through Rance’s diplomatic efforts. As for their reasoning, I think they wanted to broaden their horizons.”

“Did they know the rainforest women are nearly naked?”

“Their parents told them. But it didn’t seem to put them off.”

“Did you and Rance keep watch over the boys?”

“Oh, yeah, that was a strict requirement of their visit. And Vik and Sluggo bunked at your old place.”

“No one else has taken up fulltime residence there?”

“Nope, the place is strictly for V.I.P.s. The shaman stays there, whenever he stops by to drop off a baby.”

“But I thought Vik and Sluggo were scared of girls.”

“I thought so, too. But something must’ve happened to change their minds.”

“What?”

“Puberty, maybe? I know their voices have been changing.”

“What did the boys do during their waking hours in the rainforest?”

“They checked out the garden and the goats. And they paid their respects at the Sacred Knoll. And they sat in on Gloria’s morning school and her evening campfire story time.”

"And these activities took up their entire day?"

"Nope, they mostly hung out with other teenagers."

"I assume this was all supervised."

"Rance and I watched them every minute. And our wives kept checking up on us."

"Did the boys play any favorites?"

"Yeah, they mostly stayed with Sheela."

"But she's older than both of them."

"And the best educated of the young women, too. I suspect that was the attraction."

"With those boys, a brain is more essential than outward physical characteristics."

"Yeah, I suspect so."

"You don't suppose this is going to cause trouble, do you?"

"I'm just the babysitter. What do I know?"

"It could be something else, brother. Vik and Sluggo know Sheela, from the many times she's visited Earth Town to study with Doctor Johnson."

"Yeah, but Sheela was fully clothed then."

"True that. But Vik and Sluggo might see Sheela as a big sister, someone in whom they can confide and seek advice."

"Yeah, that makes sense."

"And Sheela has her career to consider. She can't be getting married and having kids."

"Oh, that reminds me. I meant to tell you that Doctor Johnson is preggers."

"Janis is going to have a child?"

"Yeah, and that means that when the baby comes, Sheela will have her hands full with seeing to the medical needs of two communities."

"But is it safe for Janis to have a child, at her age?"

"On Earth, it would be iffy. But here, Janis is physically in her early twenties."

"True that."

"Our benefactors threw out the rule book, when they brought us here. Who knows what lies ahead for us?"

"True that," said Andy. "Who knows?"

18—A BABY IS BORN

Sheela was nervous when it came time for Janis to deliver her child. The budding medico had been in Earth Town, three days before, in preparation. Sheela had studied library digital video discs featuring live births. And she had witnessed the nativities of her younger sisters in Brook Haven in the Forest. But this would be the first delivery where she would be in charge.

Nancy the Nurse promised to be at Sheela's side. Having given birth herself, Nancy had also assisted Janis in the delivery of Linda's baby.

Additionally, Janis would be conscious enough to talk Sheela through much of the procedure.

*****

Although the parturition went well, Sheela was nearly as exhausted as Janis was.

"The scale says five pounds, two ounces," Nancy proclaimed.

"That's small, isn't it?" Roy asked.

"Not here," Janis replied. "There's less gravity. On Earth, he would be an eight-pounder, at least."

"Have you picked out a name, yet?" Sheela inquired.

"Seth," answered Janis, beaming at her newborn.

"My paternal grandfather's first name," Roy expounded. "I think it's from the Bible. But Grandpa was named for a character on *Wagon Train*."

"*Wagon Train*?" Sheela, Nancy, and Linda queried in unison.

"It was a television show," Janis answered. "My grandparents watched it, too."

"The people portrayed on *Wagon Train* were pioneers," said Roy, "like we are: New people in a new land."

"You're going to have to take over my duties in Brook Haven in the Forest now," Janis said to Sheela. "I'm going to be pretty busy raising a child."

"But I'm not ready," Sheela begged to differ.

"I presume you are."

"Thanks, but—"

"Nancy will stop in every week, to see how you're doing."

"I appreciate that. But what if there's an emergency?"

"You've already been handling emergencies, Sheela."

"Small emergencies, yes. But what if something really big comes up?"

"You can send Mister Harrison for help. And we'll get assistance to you.

"Keep in mind," Janis pressed on, "that you've been practicing medicine for a while now. I've seen you in action, Sheela. There's nothing you can't handle. During the pioneer period, on Earth, a physician didn't have more than a horse and a buggy and a stethoscope and a little black bag of pharmaceuticals and instruments. You have a great deal more than that at your disposal."

"This might be true, but—"

"Don't forget," Nancy interposed, "you'll have Rance and Craig there. And they know a bit about medicine, too."

"I'll have to admit that Craig would be a good reference. He borrowed and read all of the textbooks, when I was done with them."

"You won't be alone, Sheela," said Janis. "Trust your friends and yourself. Everybody has to have an initiation, you know. This is yours."

"But—"

"No buts about it, girl. You're on your way. And you'll do fine."

"And we'll be able to get to the rainforest faster now," said Nancy.

"How's that?"

"Our sons are starting up a commuter airline," Linda illuminated.

"What's a commuter airline?"

"Andy says the boys can have the *Albatross II*," said Linda, "when he's not using it. So, David and Victor will be flying folks to and from Earth Town, every few days."

"How long does the journey take on the Floating Hut?"

"It's faster than the dune buggy," Nancy answered.

"And probably safer, too," said Janis, glowering at her spouse.

"Honey," Roy rose to his defense, "I drive only as fast as conditions warrant."

"All I can say, Roy, is that the ride is rather jolting."

"But the commuter airline is smooth sailing," said Nancy, "according to David and Victor. And they won't need the bicycle and the water tank on board, so their removal will make the *Albatross II* roomier and lighter."

"By the way," said Linda, "how did Victor and David conduct themselves in the women's village?"

"They were on their best behavior," answered Sheela. "And they made a few conquests among my friends."

"But nothing serious," a hopeful Nancy wished aloud.

"It is serious," said Sheela, "on the part of my sisters. But not with the boys."

"Why did they make the trip?" Janis asked.

"As you know," Sheela replied, "Victor and David have lived on the grassland for all of their lives. And most of the trees they saw were in the fruit and nut orchards here. And those aren't big trees, compared to a rainforest."

"I get it," said Linda. "Until they picked up the wicker panels at the rainforest, they'd never seen big trees, except in books."

"That's right," said Sheela. "And when they rode on the Floating Hut with the god, they saw big trees from up high. But they'd never been walking beneath big trees."

"Then the big trees were the big attraction?" Nancy asked.

"That's my belief. They roamed through the woods with Rance. And they climbed big trees. The bigger, the better. And they asked me the name and medical use of every plant they saw."

"Then," said Linda, "they're still boys. Big boys. But still boys."

"I'd say they were boys," Sheela answered. "Boy botanists."

"Yes," said Linda. "Our sons are sincere scientists, at heart."

Nancy raised a forefinger. "It's not just that David and Victor are too young to get serious about girls. They have a job to do here."

"What's that?" asked Sheela.

"They have to be big brothers and role models," Nancy replied.

"Yes," said Sheela. "I'm sure they'll be a big help with Seth."

"But not just with Seth," said Nancy. "Linda and I found out we're pregnant again."

19—THE LAST ELBASTAK

Ginger (the golden-brown, short-haired, mid-size mongrel dog) rarely strayed from Aleesa's side and accompanied her on every hunt. It was on one of these tracking forays—in company with Gloria and Rance—that Ginger ceased stalking and stood stock-still. Aleesa, Gloria, and Rance, who were trailing close behind the canine, also froze.

Ginger's ears twitched—and she dashed off to her right. The humans wordlessly followed.

Twenty yards distant, in a circular and treeless area, a gruesome tableau greeted them. Two bloody and deceased elbastak lay on their sides, a few feet from each other.

Ginger was on her stomach; she was licking something.

"What happened here?" Gloria inquired, in English.

Rance studied the ground for a few seconds, prior to answering: "A fight to the finish."

"Why?"

"A mother, protecting her cubs from an adult male."

"Why would a male cat kill kittens?"

"It's not uncommon," Rance prosaically replied, "for a male predator animal to do something like this. No one knows why. Some say that it's instinct. Some say that it's jealousy. It could be that it's temporary insanity."

"Where are the kittens?"

"Two of them are dead. Ginger is comforting the sole survivor."

"Why is Ginger licking the kitten?"

"I reckon Ginger's maternal feelings kicked in."

"The kitten's eyes aren't open, yet."

"The cub is pretty young. And I doubt that it's weaned."

Ginger peered up at Rance.

"Do you want me to carry the cub home for you?" the hunter asked the dog.

Ginger sat and panted, as though in answer.

Rance carefully picked up the cub and held it to his chest. "You two can continue with the hunt," he said to Gloria and Aleesa, in the woodlander tongue. "Ginger and I are going home."

Gloria looked to Aleesa.

"We should go with Rance and Ginger," the chieftain said.

Gloria and Aleesa fell in behind Rance, with Ginger leading the way. At a hurried pace, they were back to the borough within ten minutes.

Rance deposited the cub onto a mat in Aleesa's hut. "It might drink goat milk. But we'll need a nipple to feed it."

"I know just the thing," said Gloria. "I'll be back in two shakes of a goat's tail."

The canine curled her body around the shivering kitten.

"Ginger is trying to warm the little one," Aleesa said, in the woodlander tongue.

"It seems we have another member of the family," Rance averred. "And I doubt that Ginger will be hunting with us for a while."

"Ginger is a mother now."

"And the cub is a female, so she will fit in nicely here."

"If you say so," the chieftain hesitantly answered.

"Those cats were the first ones I have seen for a long while."

"I believe the cats might be dying out."

"We are in accord, Aleesa."

"What if this one is the last of its kind?"

"The last of the elbastak," Rance commented, in English. "That's an awful sad sentiment."

"I never liked those black creepers," said Aleesa, in the woodlander tongue. "But I feel sorrow for this little one."

"I know what you mean," Rance replied. "I do not know if the cub will survive. Nor do I know if the cub will grow up to be, uh, I cannot come up with the woodlander word for *tame*."

"What is *tame*?"

"*Tame* is gentle. Like Ginger is gentle."

"I see," said Aleesa, in English. "Perhaps Ginger can raise her right. She can raise her to be tame."

The hunter grinned. "Where did you hear the phrase: *Raise her right*?"

"Janis says it. She has been telling the mothers to raise their children right. I believe I now know what she means. Janis wants the children to be tame."

"All children ought to be tame. But few of them are."

"Do you believe Ginger can raise her right?"

"It would not be the first time that an animal of one kind," Rance answered, "raised an animal of another kind, and did it right."

"I have never heard of such a thing. But then, you have more experience than I do."

"That's because I once lived in a bigger world," said Rance, "with a passel of animals."

"I keep meaning to ask you, my husband: Where is this world?"

"I have no idea. And now I wonder if it ever existed."

"Sometimes, my husband, you speak strangely."

"I reckon I do."

"I got it," said Gloria, as she entered the hut. "I filled one of Sheela's latex gloves with goat milk."

"But how will the goat milk get out of the glove and into the cub?" Rance asked.

Gloria produced a sewing needle. "This might do the trick."

She pricked the end of one of the glove fingers.

A bead of white exuded from the aperture, and Gloria knelt to offer the latex digit to the cub.

"Rub a little milk on her nose," Rance prompted.

Gloria followed suit, and the cub licked her own nose.

"I think the kitten likes it," said Gloria.

"Now put the glove finger on the cub's mouth."

"She's taking the nipple," said Gloria.

"How did you know this would work?" the chieftain asked the hunter.

"I was raised with animals."

"I thought you said you were raised with older sisters," Aleesa recollected.

"Don't say it," the seamstress warned the hunter.

Rance suppressed a snigger. "My sisters taught me this trick."

"You can learn much from females," said Aleesa.

"Truer words were never spoken," Rance replied.

20—GINGER AND SNAP

The Elbastak cub did more than survive; she flourished—on account of the constant attention paid to her by Aleesa and her sorority.

As to that, Ginger never left the kitten and stayed in almost constant physical contact with her.

Rance dubbed the cub "Snap." And the name stuck—although no one in Brook Haven in the Forest, except for Craig and Gloria, understood the confection connection between Ginger and Snap.

When Snap took her first tentative steps outside Aleesa's hut, Ginger was at her side. The dog often seemed to sense what Snap wanted to do—and when she wanted to do it.

As Snap grew in size, and her nose drew her to strings of dried fish, which the women hung by communal serving tables, Ginger made certain that Snap had access to all of the desiccated tilapia she wanted to nibble—although Ginger found piscatorial odors to be objectionable.

As for Snap, she mimicked Ginger in every other respect.

"Snap reckons she's a dog," Rance said to Craig. "Snap trots like Ginger does. She scratches herself like Ginger does. She pants like Ginger does. She even chaws on bones like Ginger does. Snap doesn't act like a cat at all."

"Yeah, I can see that," Craig answered. "Ginger is Snap's solitary frame of reference. Snap knows she's not a person, because she goes around on all fours. She knows she's not a goat, because the goats shy away from her. She's never seen another elbastak. Not even her mother. And that leaves Ginger as her ideal."

"How do you reckon the damsels from the fisher-folk hangout will react," Rance asked, "when they see an elbastak slinking around the premises?"

"It'll probably blow their minds."

"Why do those damsels come here, anyhow? They never enter the *barrio*. They just stay out there in the bushes and watch."

With a shrug, Craig replied: "Beats me. The shaman tells me they're the relatives of women here. Maybe they're too ashamed to show their mugs."

"They must know that we can see them."

"The shaman told them they'd be invisible, provided they stayed far enough away."

"Why did he tell them that?"

"The shaman has his ways and reasons. And he ends up being right in the end. I don't bother to question him anymore."

"That *hombre* must be getting up in years."

"Yeah, but I have no idea how old he is. And I notice he moves more slowly than he used to."

"And that's another thing."

"What?"

"I've watched all of the damsels here get older. The kids are growing up, the teens are becoming young damsels, and the young damsels are becoming middle-aged and elderly."

"Yeah?"

"But not your wife. Dora seems to be as young as when I first met her."

Craig turned away. "It must be your imagination."

"Dora hasn't aged an iota. I'm sure of it. And I have a theory."

Craig held his breath. "What's that?"

"There's something in those leaves she chaws on, *amigo*. No one else here chaws on those leaves, except for Koree. I reckon those leaves have special powers. I reckon they retard aging."

Craig relaxed. "Maybe you're onto something there."

"Have you ever tried those leaves, *amigo*? They're bitter."

"Yeah, I know what you mean. They're an acquired taste, all right."

"Aleesa won't touch the leaves, either."

"Do you want Aleesa to stay young?"

"Negative, *amigo*."

"Really?"

"I've given it some thought," said Rance. "It's not natural that you and I stay young. It's not the way of the world. This world, or any other. It keeps me in touch with what's what, to see people age naturally."

"What do you mean?"

"A passel of things have happened to me, since I got zapped across the universe by the star hoppers. I live under two moons and next door to dinosaurs. At times, it's so unreal that I look to hold onto something that makes a lick of sense."

"I think I know what you mean, my friend. Human beings require a grasp of realism. It's what keeps them sane, in an insane world."

"And this world seems more insane, with each passing day."

"Yeah," said Craig. "But friends are the key to sanity. And you and I seem to be blessed with friends. Here's hoping they'll carry us through."

"Here's hoping, *amigo*."

21—PERMIAN WORLD

Craig was loping toward the showers and medical facility one morning, when he spied the *Albatross II* on the prairie horizon.

After Andy set down the aircraft near the border of the rainforest, Koree ran to Craig and slapped his outstretched hand—a familiar convention with those two—and scurried into the jungle.

"Koree seems happy," Craig said to Andy.

"Yes," the deity answered. "It was another successful outing."

"You found a third island?"

"Yes, with another set of flora and fauna. I haven't fully confirmed it in the library, yet. But I'm supposing the island is a Permian World."

"Permian?" Craig reiterated. "You mean dimetrodons and swamp forests?"

"Yes, not a dinosaur anywhere. You would've hated it."

"Yeah, but still, dimetrodons. Like in the old science-fiction movies: Gigantic iguanas with fins glued to their backs."

"Yes, that describes a dimetrodon."

"Anything else?"

"Let me consult my checklist here." Andy pulled a notebook from his back pocket. "According to the foldout I brought with us, we also saw gorgonopsians, dicynodonts, cynodonts, moschops, and diplocaulus. All in all, a fantastical menagerie."

"Wait a minute. You had a foldout of the Permian era with you on your flight. Were you expecting to find a Permian World?"

"I had a hunch. The first big land animals made the scene in the Permian, 298 million years ago. And that gave way to the Triassic, 251 million years ago. And that gave way to the Jurassic, 201 million years ago."

"Yeah, that's the way I remember it, too. But you think there's a pattern here?"

"I'll tell you one thing, brother. These three islands are in a straight line and nearly equidistant from each other. I suppose, on the next flight out, if I aim west-northwest, along that same line, I'll run into a Cretaceous World, which was ushered in 145 million years ago and ended 66 million years ago."

"You're serious?"

"As a pimple on prom night. But, for the moment, this is nothing but a hypothesis."

"Did you tell Koree?"

"Yes, she's all for another adventure."

"But did you tell her what animals lived in the cretaceous?"

"No."

"You realize there were T-Rexes and velociraptors and triceratops."

"Yes."

"Do you think she could handle those?"

"She handled an Allosaurus."

"Yeah, but a Tyrannosaurus rex. That's bigger than an Allosaurus. And there was Giganotosaurus. And that was at least as big as a Tyrannosaurus rex. And Spinosaurus was the biggest carnivore of them all. They were all there in the Cretaceous."

"I'll fly high, brother. And keep in mind, it's a hypothesis. I could be all wrong about it."

"I have to admit, my friend, that there's some fairly outlandish stuff going on here."

"True that."

"What could be the rationale?"

"Perchance it's a zoo?"

"Yeah, maybe."

"But I'm supposing it's more than that."

"You have another hypothesis?"

"I'm working on one. I just need more input."

"That's the great tragedy of science."

"What is?"

"The slaying of a beautiful hypothesis, by ugly facts."

"Ah, yes. Thomas Henry Huxley said that, didn't he? And he was right. But, sometimes, you know, the beautiful hypothesis lives on."

"Yeah, keep me posted, please."

"You can depend on it, brother."

22—EARTH TOWN ADJUNCTS

Nancy and Linda gave birth, a week apart. And since Nancy was unable to assist during her own labor, Sheela filled in—and the woodlander M.D. stayed on for Linda's delivery, too.

The infants, both boys, were named Jonathan and Joshua—rapidly shortened by Earth Town denizens to Jon and Josh.

Gloria put her prize sewing students to work making mithrill clothes for Seth and Jon and Josh, since there weren't enough hand-me-downs from Vik and Sluggo to go around.

Vik and Sluggo helped their parents as much as they could. The teenagers looked forward to acting as brothers and unofficial uncles to Seth and Jon and Josh.

Andy took over the commuter airline duties of Vik and Sluggo for a few weeks. Then, the boys helped him reinstall the bicycle and water tank and dried food for another overseas flight with Koree.

This was also the season for births among the goats and antelope, which kept Chris the Farmer busy. But Chris knew that he could depend on his neighbors to help him out.

The goats and antelope no longer stayed in pens. Decades of domestication had rendered these animals wholly dependent upon humans. They were treated, and acted, as pets—even to the extent of coming when called by their individual names. And there were no plains predators from which to protect these tame vertebrates.

Feral antelope avoided Earth Town, so there was no intra-species interaction. Antelope hunts had to wait until a wild herd came within a day's hiking distance. This being the situation, such stalking parties were few and far between—and involved extended reconnaissance.

Yet, there was no scarcity of meat. With the addendum of new fruits and vegetables and nuts and legumes, from seeds and saplings supplied by Craig's confidential quartermaster, there was also less need or desire to eat meat.

If a carnivore craving was in the offing, it could be satisfied by a visit to Brook Haven in the Forest for pork and venison. And Earth Town citizenry continued to make fishing junkets to the northern river for tilapia.

Hank the Baker and Frank the Cook were talking about going into business and planned to introduce a specialty eatery to serve daily breakfasts to the locals. They were thinking of calling it *Hank's and Frank's*.

Designs were also in the offing to construct more residences for the young people to live in, when they grew older.

And, since bags of cement (to mix for concrete) kept popping up in Orv the Mason's stock supplies, structural material was readily available.

"This town keeps growing," Linda once mentioned to Janis.

"Yes," the physician replied. "It's a good thing we have plenty of acreage."

"Remember when we used to call this place a camp?"

"And now it's Earth Town."

"Do you think it could ever be Earth City?"

"I wouldn't want that. I like the small-shire charm, don't you?"

"Sure, I do. But you can't stop progress."

"But you can slow it down a little. I don't want to pick up the pace."

"But that will be out of our hands, you know."

"Yes, our kids will be making the decisions someday."

"And their kids, too."

"I don't want to think about that."

"I know what you mean. But these things take care of themselves."

"Yes, we can but watch and wait."

23—PLEISTOCENE WORLD

Craig was again on hand, at the edge of the rainforest, when the *Albatross II* loomed in the early morning sky.

Koree ran past Craig, slapping his outstretched hand, as usual.

"Another good outing?" Craig asked Andy.

"We found two more islands," the god replied.

"Was Cretaceous World there?"

"In all its glory. And another seventy-or-so miles beyond Cretaceous World was Pleistocene World."

"You're kidding me."

"I kid you not, brother. Pleistocene World: Home of saber-toothed tigers and mastodons and eohippus, the dawn horse."

"Pleistocene World," said Craig, "which kicked in two and a half million years ago, and ended about twelve thousand years ago?"

"The very same, brother. We saw wooly mammoths and wooly rhinoceroses. We saw ground sloths and cave bears. We saw dire wolves and cave lions."

"Lions and tigers and bears, oh, my."

"You bet, brother."

"Did you see any humans?"

"No, there were no humans. It was just Koree and I and the Pleistocene flora and fauna."

"Why do you believe there are no humans there? I know they existed in considerable numbers during the Pleistocene."

"My hypothesis is that humans were the cause of animal extinctions in the Pleistocene."

"They probably were. But what are you driving at?"

"It's another hypothesis I've been working on. I'll let you know when I have it all figured out. But do you recollect that I told you that Vik and Sluggo had found five satellites, with the telescope you got them? And the satellites were in geosynchronous orbits?"

"Yeah, I do."

"And do you recollect that I told you that the satellites are in an arc, evenly spaced, from west-northwest to east-southeast. And one of those satellites is directly above us?"

"Yeah, I do."

"Well, I'm supposing that those satellites are hovering above these other four islands, in addition to our own."

"You think our benefactors put eyes in the sky to keep tabs on the five islands?"

"That's my supposition."

"Hmmm," Craig hummed.

"It makes sense, brother. Our benefactors are a curious lot."

"Do you envisage further exploration?"

"No, two islands, in any direction, is the maximum flying limit for the *Albatross II*. And Vik and Sluggo will be ferrying passengers between Earth Town and the women's burg, from now on."

"That's not a bad idea, my friend. The boys will probably have a lot of customers every month. The dune buggy accommodates two people. But the *Albatross II* can probably carry four or five, can't it?"

"Yes, that's the way I see it. Vik and Sluggo are going to jettison the water tank and bicycle again. That will make a big difference."

"And since you own the airline, you can retire a rich man."

"Yes," said Andy. "I have that to look forward to, in a few hundred years."

24—FAREWELL TO LODA

The shaman and his apprentice came to a halt next to a small marsh in the rainforest. The older man grasped the shoulders of the younger man.

"Loda," the shaman said, "our journey together is coming to an end."

"What do you mean?" his alarmed apprentice inquired.

"It is nearly time for you to assume the mantle of the shaman, Loda."

"But I am not prepared, Master. I am not ready."

"I disagree with you, Loda. You are prepared. And you are ready. You know all that I know."

"I do not know how to hear the wind talk to me, Master."

"This is something I cannot teach you, Loda. It is something you will learn for yourself."

"I cannot read the stars, Master."

"This ability, too, will be yours, Loda, if you are patient."

"I cannot yet interpret the jewels, Master, when they are thrown onto the leather skin."

"Again, Loda, this skill will be yours. Remember what I told you to do. And be patient."

“The Tree Spirit has never spoken to me, Master.”

“Ah,” soughed the shaman, “as to that, the Tree Spirit will speak to you today.”

“It will?”

“We are standing beside the very tree inhabited by the Tree Spirit.”

“We are?”

“We are, Loda. The sound of the Tree Spirit has changed, incidentally. I do not know why.”

“What must I do for the Tree Spirit to speak to me, Master?”

“Listen,” replied the shaman.

“Loda,” barked a baritone brogue.

The apprentice looked about, but saw no one except his master.

“Can you hear the Tree Spirit?” the shaman asked.

“I heard someone call my name, Master.”

“Then answer,” said the shaman.

“I am here,” said Loda.

“I am the Tree Spirit,” came a response.

“I cannot see you, Tree Spirit,” Loda said.

“That is because I cannot be seen, Loda.”

“Oh,” said the apprentice, as he processed this reply. “What do you want of me, Tree Spirit?”

"We are getting acquainted today, Loda."

"Oh," was all Loda could think to say.

"Whenever you need something of me, Loda, come to this place and call for me. I shall answer."

"Is that all I must do, Tree Spirit?"

"Be sure you are not followed, Loda. If there is anyone else within the range of your hearing, I shall be silent. It is with you, solely, that I shall speak."

"What might I need from you, Tree Spirit?"

"You might never need anything, Loda. But I might need to talk to you about something. If that happens, I shall call for you in your hut. When you hear me, you are to come here, and we shall speak."

"What could I give to you, Tree Spirit?"

"It could be anything, Loda. I might need you to be somewhere, or do something."

"Oh, well, I can do that, Tree Spirit."

"Say goodbye to the Tree Spirit, Loda," the shaman said.

"Goodbye, Tree Spirit," said Loda.

"Goodbye, Loda. It was nice meeting you and talking with you."

The shaman waved for Loda to follow him into the rainforest.

"Now you have spoken to the Tree Spirit," said the shaman, as they moved through the woodland. "The rest will naturally follow."

"I thought it would be a more glorious experience, Master, to speak with the Tree Spirit."

"Anticipation commonly leads to disappointment, Loda. But disappointment builds character."

"What is character, Master?"

"Character, Loda, is strength and courage. Character is how you handle having power. Character is how you treat those who cannot help you, or those who cannot harm you."

"I see, Master. Character, then, is a good thing to have."

"It is a very good thing to have, Loda."

"Character is strength and courage, Master?"

"Truly, it is, Loda. But keep in mind that physical courage is common enough, whereas moral courage is rare. Always do the right thing, no matter how hard it is to do."

"If I have moral courage, Master, I shall be a good shaman?"

"If you always do the right thing, Loda, the just thing, the honorable thing, you will be a good shaman. And your people will benefit from your actions."

"Do I know everything I need to know to be a good shaman, Master?"

"There is one more thing, Loda."

"What is that, Master?"

"If, every day, you care enough, Loda, you will make a difference."

"That is all, Master?"

"Caring means much, Loda. And, in the fullness of passing days, you will come to realize this."

25—THE SHAMAN GOES WEST

The sun was rising as the chieftain and the shaman greeted each other outside the medicine man's hut.

"Why is your bedroll draped upon your shoulder?" the chieftain inquired.

"I must make a journey," the shaman replied.

"You expect to stay overnight somewhere?"

"This is my intention."

"That seems a long journey—"

"For someone my age," the shaman finished the chieftain's thought.

Paul grunted.

"Do your wives remain quarrelsome, My Chieftain?"

"They are no longer quarrelsome. Emma is still upset about giving up Sara. But, with the birth of her second child, she seems happier."

"Do not be concerned about Sara, My Chieftain. She is in a better place. And she will do good things there."

"Aleesa said she would look after Sara."

"And she will, My Chieftain. You can depend on it."

Paul grunted.

"You have a new son, My Chieftain. Have you named him, yet?"

"That is your job."

"We are in accord, My Chieftain. But, you know, I consult with the parents first."

"Emma wants to call him Koltun."

"A good name, My Chieftain. Koltun it is, then."

Paul grunted.

"And you are expecting another child by Kora?"

"Kora expects to give birth within a few days."

"Are the elders behaving to your satisfaction?"

"They are behaving to my satisfaction. I do not know why. But I am not looking a gift goat in the mouth."

"This is sagacious."

"You foresaw that my wives would cease being quarrelsome and the elders would cease being an irritation to me."

"It was foretold by the stars."

Paul grunted. "I believe there was more involved. But who am I to question my shaman?"

"This is also sagacious."

"But, if you did have a hand in it, I thank you."

The shaman reached up and patted the chieftain's herculean chest. "You are most welcome."

"When will you come back from your journey?"

"This will be my final journey. I shall not be coming back."

Paul's eyes grew wider. "That is why you summoned me? To tell me you are leaving forever?"

"That is why."

"I do not understand."

"It is the way of the world, My Chieftain. People grow old and die."

"You cannot die."

"Ah, but I must die, My Chieftain. We all must."

"But how do you know you are dying?"

"I have my ways. But be not dismayed. Loda will make a fine shaman. I have trained him long and well."

"Loda will doubtless be a fine shaman. But he will not be you. There will never be your like again. You are the greatest man I know."

A tear trickled down the shaman's cheek. "I love you, too, Paul."

"I do not have the words," the chieftain said, haltingly.

"You have spoken fine words already, My Chieftain. If anyone asks, tell them I have gone toward the setting sun, never to return."

"How long is your journey?"

"A few more days."

"Have you told Loda?"

"I told Loda I was leaving. But I did not tell him when, exactly. I was hoping you would tell him for me. Loda will need your steady hand to keep him from faltering."

"My steady hand?"

"You are the greatest chieftain of them all. I have foreseen this. And, if you ever require assistance, do not hesitate to call upon the angels of the God in the Sky."

"You mean, Rance and Craig?"

"Rance and Craig will do anything for you. And so will Dora. Call on them, when all others let you down."

"I shall keep this in mind."

"Then, My Chieftain, I shall be leaving."

"May I walk with you?"

"There is no need. And you will be too busy."

"Busy? Doing what?"

A moment later, Paul heard Borg calling him.

"What do you think he wants?" asked the chieftain.

"I know what he wants, My Chieftain. But I do not want to spoil the surprise."

Paul's eyes widened again. "It is Kora."

"I believe so."

"She has given me a child."

"I believe so."

"This is a bad way to say farewell."

"I detest long goodbyes, Paul."

Borg bellowed once more.

"I must go," said the chieftain.

"As must I," said the shaman.

"May your journey be pleasant."

"And may your days be full of happiness, My Chieftain."

Paul's eyes welled with tears.

"Your wife and child await you," said the shaman.

"I know I must go."

"And so must I," said the shaman, while he strode toward the trees. "Think of me sometimes."

"Always," replied the chieftain. "I shall always have you in my heart."

"Tell them that I vanished into the morning mists," the shaman said, before he vanished into the morning mists.

26—THE SHAMAN BOOKS A FLIGHT

It was shortly after sundown when the shaman showed up at Brook Haven in the Forest. Craig was on hand to greet him.

"I would like to ride in the Floating Hut," the shaman said.

"I believe this can be arranged," Craig replied. "In fact, the Floating Hut is due to arrive at the edge of the rainforest tomorrow."

"I would like to ride on the Floating Hut to Earth Town."

"Your wish is my command, Shaman."

"I have never been to Earth Town."

"I think you will find pleasure in seeing it."

"And I would like to talk with the God in the Sky," the shaman said, "while I am in Earth Town."

"I shall see what I can do."

"The God in the Sky has completed his journeys of exploration?"

"The God in the Sky has done so."

"I have another request," said the shaman. "But I must ask it of your chieftain."

"My chieftain will want you to spend the night, of course."

"It is more than that."

"And you ought to have something to eat and drink, after your long journey."

"It is more than that."

"Shall we go to her hut?"

"If you do not mind."

"Perhaps some water from the creek, before we go?"

"This would be most appreciated."

As they ambled toward the meandering stream, Craig inquired: "Do you want me to assist you with your request to my chieftain?"

"This would be welcomed," replied the shaman. "It is an unusual and, perhaps impossible, request."

"Impossible?"

"The request might be against the law of your chieftain."

"I do not understand. Why might it be against the law?"

The shaman knelt at the creek and cupped his hands in the flowing water. "I do not know the laws of your chieftain."

"We can but ask."

The shaman sipped the translucent liquid in his hands. "Ah, your water is always so delicious. And so cool."

Craig waggled a thumb upstream. "The origin of the creek is deep under the ground."

"It burbles up, I call to mind."

"That it does."

"Would that laws were always so refreshing."

"I must confess," said Craig, "that I do not know all of the laws of my chieftain. I did not even know I got married, until the ritual was over."

"I call that to mind, too." The shaman dipped his hands into the water again. "It is a most amusing anecdote."

"Perhaps if you told me what you want, I could—"

"Welcome to our homestead," Aleesa interjected.

Craig hadn't heard his chieftain approach, but the shaman seemed unruffled by her abrupt manifestation and drank again.

"You have had a long walk," Aleesa resumed. "Please stay in our guest hut, as you always have done."

"Your hospitality is greatly appreciated," the shaman answered.

"I overheard you say that you have a request of me."

The shaman struggled to his feet and replied: "It is a most unusual request."

"Please," said the chieftain, "let us all sit here by the creek."

"Your suggestion is greatly appreciated," said the shaman. "I am quite spent."

"The shaman wants to visit Earth Town," Craig put in.

"I shall be gone for a long while," said the shaman.

"Why are you going to Earth Town?" Aleesa queried.

"I have never been there. And I have heard good things about the place."

"It is a good place to visit," said Aleesa. "But I would not want to live there."

"I also want to see the land beyond the mountains. Do you think the God in the Sky would take me there in his Floating Hut?"

"I can see no reason why he would not," answered the chieftain. "But what do you require of me?"

"When I come back from my journey in the air, I would like to remain here."

"You may do so," said Aleesa.

"Forever," affixed the shaman.

"Forever?" Craig jumped in.

"I would like to be buried in the Sacred Knoll."

"You would like to be buried in the sacred knoll?" an incredulous Craig inquired.

"I know it is an unusual request," the shaman acknowledged, "and it might be against your law."

"But why would you not want to be buried in your own homestead?" Craig asked.

"I cannot say. The wind said this to me. I thought it was unusual. But the wind has never misled me. Is my request against your law?"

“I am the chieftain,” replied Aleesa. “I am the law.”

“What is your law?”

“I am compelled to honor your request. That is my word. And that is my law.”

Craig gaped at his chieftain, but said nothing.

“You see,” Aleesa explicated to Craig and the shaman, “the wind spoke to me, also.”

27—ALEESA'S EXPLANATION

When the shaman was watered and fed and bedded down for the evening, Aleesa said to Craig: "Let us go to the garden."

The electrician silently accompanied the chieftain.

"A week before Zeena passed away," Aleesa prefaced, "she summoned Dora and me to her hut. Has your wife mentioned this?"

"Dora has said nothing of this matter."

Aleesa smiled. "My sister can keep a secret. But I feel that now it would be appropriate for me to tell you this secret. But you must not say anything about it to anyone else."

"I guarantee it."

"When Zeena first sat down to talk with the shaman, many cycles of the stars ago, there was something in his talking which sounded familiar."

The chieftain paused, prior to going on. "When Zeena was a little girl, she saw a young man come to this place. Back then, it was a tiny glade. The young man came, with every filling of the moons. He brought food and seeds and hunting weapons and many other items necessary for survival and comfort."

The chieftain assayed the herbarium under the moonlight. "The seeds the young man brought were the beginnings of the big garden we have today. The food the young man brought kept

Zeena and her parents alive, when they otherwise would have perished. The young man even brought two goats, a male and a female, which are the progenitors of the flock we have today. And, on occasion, the young man transported light-skinned children who had been left out to die. Zeena later learned from her parents that the young man had led her parents to this glade, which he had discovered in his wanderings.

"But, on one visit, the young man said he was being followed and could no longer safely come to this glade."

"Why was he being followed?"

"The young man said he was suspected of knowing the whereabouts of Zeena and her parents. And he was suspected of saving abandoned children. He said he did not want to stop saving the children. But he could not risk imperiling Zeena and her parents and their little ones.

"By then, Zeena was old enough to make the walk to the stronghold of the fishermen. So, she spoke up and said that she and her mother would go to the place where the children were abandoned, and rescue them.

"To this, the young man pledged that he would place a beacon in the sky, whenever a child was being abandoned. He said the beacon would be a plume of red smoke which would rise above the treetops.

"So, every day, Zeena climbed the tallest tree in this area and looked for the red smoke. Whenever Zeena saw the red smoke, she and her mother made their way to the place of abandonment, and rescued the children. And, later, we sisters took over this duty."

Craig's eyes blithely wrinkled. "I think I know who the young man was."

Aleesa canted her head. "It took Zeena many cycles of the stars to make this connection. But she finally recognized that the talking of the young man and the talking of the shaman, although altered by age, were the same."

"Then, the shaman is responsible for keeping Zeena and her parents alive, and for saving all of the women here."

"We are in accord. Without the shaman, there would be no Brook Haven in the Forest. He was both our founder and our continuing savior. So, if the shaman wants to be buried here, he will be buried here. It is the least that we can do, I should think, in gratitude."

"Do you believe the shaman might be related to Zeena?"

"I cannot say. I prefer to think of the shaman as a man who saw the right thing to do, and did it. As my husband would say, in your *lingo*: 'He walked the talk.'"

"Yeah," Craig answered, in English. "That pretty much says it all."

28—A FINAL JOURNEY

The succeeding day, Craig led the shaman to the bus stop, adjacent to the showers and medical facility, at the fringe of the flatlands. As they reached the terminal, the *Albatross II* was disgorging Tim, Phil, Barney, George, and Bailey.

"Hello, Rance's Rangers," Craig greeted the men. "The first of us Earthlings to make contact with the rainforest civilization."

"We're the stuff of history," Barney replied.

"A footnote of idle gossip, you mean," said George.

"Who remembers us as Rance's Rangers," Bailey said to Craig, "except for you and Rance?"

"Back then," Phil reminisced, "it took us an entire day to hike here."

"And these days," Tim amended, "we fly here in a few hours. Who knew that would happen?"

"Who, indeed?" was Craig's riposte.

The emeritus Rance's Rangers respectfully saluted the shaman, who reciprocated in kind.

And, with that, the quintet faded into the foliage.

"How much is the fare?" Craig asked Sluggo, pointing to the shaman and himself.

"Since it's you fine gentlemen," the youth replied, "the ride is on the house."

"We really ought to come up with a system of coinage and currency someday," Craig jested.

"Why?" Sluggo parried, in earnest. "Have you ever heard anyone squawk about the existing system of barter?"

"I can't say I have."

"Keep it simple," Sluggo advocated. "That's what Rance says."

"Yeah, that's usually a solid methodology."

"Who's your friend?" Vik inquired, as the shaman inspected the *Albatross II* in awed quietude.

"A fellow I picked up last night. He wants to palaver with the God in the Sky."

"You're beginning to talk like Rance," said Sluggo.

"I reckon we all are," Craig answered.

*****

The shaman remained on the balcony of the *Albatross II* throughout the flight from the rainforest to Earth Town.

The boys insisted that both the shaman and Craig wear safety harnesses. This was a prudent course of action, Craig opined, in that the shaman was acting like a small child, whooping it up and dancing about, for much of the trip.

"Sort of spry for a senior citizen, isn't he?" Sluggo observed.

"Yeah," Craig replied. "I'm impressed, too. He seemed pretty tuckered out last night."

"How old is he?"

"He told me once that he's seen one hundred cycles of the stars. And this was a while back. So, he's quite probably a centenarian, in Earth years."

"Exceptional," was all Sluggo could think to reply.

*****

Upon alighting at Earth Town, Craig thanked the boys for the ride, and led the shaman to Andy's Quonset hut—which had once belonged to Craig.

The shaman verbally marveled when the door opened inward—putting Craig in mind of the reaction his wife had evinced, on seeing her first door in operation. In fact, it had been this very door.

Craig left the God in the Sky and the shaman to converse, while he rustled up food and drink for them at *Hank's and Frank's*, a new augmentation to Earth Town.

Hank the Baker and Frank the Cook had gone into the breakfast business. And *Hank's and Frank's* had become the morning meeting place for the Earthling residents.

"You're our first takeout customer," Hank disclosed.

"Ever," Frank complemented.

"I have a couple of friends visiting," Craig revealed, "and they're late risers."

"Yup," said Frank. "We saw you fly in. Who's the oldster?"

"That's the shaman of the fisher folk. This is his first visit to Earth Town."

"Heh," Hank honked. "It sure took him long enough to get here."

"He's a busy fellow. But he finally got a few days of vacation."

"Vacation?" Frank exclaimed. "What's that?"

"Don't you fellows get away to the rainforest?"

"Oh, sure," said Hank. "But someone has to run this place while we're gone. And when we get to the jungle, our wives put us to work."

"Yeah," Craig commiserated. "That's tough."

"Hey," said Hank, "if I never said it before, I sure appreciate that you and Rance come here every year to help with the harvest."

"Yup," said Frank. "We need all the hands we can hire."

"Well, it gets me out of doing chores for the missus."

"Yeah," said Hank. "Married life is rough."

"Roger that," said Frank.

"I hear Earth Town has two more tenants on the way."

"Huh?" said Hank.

"I hear Linda and Nancy are having babies again," Craig clarified.

"Oh, yeah," said Hank. "The more, the merrier. We might even have to put up new housing."

"Where do Vik and Sluggo reside now?"

"Vik lives in his dad's old place," Frank answered. "You know, Chris moved in with Linda. And Sluggo lives in his dad's old place, since Dan moved in with Nancy."

"And Roy moved in with Janis," said Hank. "When Seth is old enough, he'll be bunking at his dad's old place."

"Order's up," Frank annunciated. "You'll be taking this back to Andy's place, uh, I mean your old place?"

"Yeah."

"You know," said Hank, "Andy has become our best customer."

"I did not know that."

"Yup," said Frank. "Andy is big on our doughnuts."

"Doughnuts and coffee," said Hank.

Craig peeked into the paper sack. "I see the doughnuts. But where's the coffee?"

"I'll deliver it in person," said Frank. "It's a perk. But, like I said, Andy is our best customer."

"And Andy says we have you to thank for our coffee shrubs," said Hank.

"And the chocolate bushes," said Frank.

Craig winked. "I know a guy."

"Well," said Hank, "we thank him, too."

"How much do I owe you?"

"It's free of charge," Hank bantered. "I have a weakness for coffee, myself."

"And I have a weakness for chocolate," said Frank.

"Don't we all," Craig replied.

"And," said Hank, "Andy says the coffee plants you got us are Arabica."

"Yeah. *Coffea arabica* is the sweetest coffee. And, when Arabica is grown in the shade, it's even sweeter."

"I didn't know that," said Frank.

"I didn't, either," said Craig, "until I did a little research in the library."

"It's a good thing we brought those books with us," said Hank.

"Yeah," said Craig. "A little foresight makes a big difference."

"You know," said Frank, "we didn't bring those books. They were here when we landed."

"Yeah," said Hank. "But all the same."

"Yeah," his two companions chorused. "All the same."

29—THE GLITTERING GODS

The shaman took much delight in his doughnut and got a big kick out of his cup of coffee.

"Our friend will be awake all night," Andy said to Craig, in the woodlander tongue (to be polite), while Craig poured the shaman a second cup from an official signature-model *Hank's & Frank's* returnable thermos.

"Maybe I should have educated the shaman concerning caffeine," Craig replied.

The medicine man seemed oblivious to the conversation, so Craig kept speaking in English.

"Then, you two will be flying off to Dinosaur Land?"

"Not right away," said Andy. "Vik and Sluggo have a few more flights to make with the *Albatross II*. And then, we'll have to re-install the water tank and the bicycle and set in a store of food. And Koree will have to come out of retirement."

"You'll need Koree," said Craig.

"I couldn't do it without her," Andy replied.

"Do you want to come with us?" the shaman queried, in English.

"You know our language?" Craig asked the shaman.

"Rance has been teaching me your *lingo*."

"That fellow certainly gets around," said Craig.

"True that," said Andy.

"How long will you two be gone?" Craig asked Andy, in the woodlander tongue.

"I intend to take a shorter route than before," the deity replied, "and keep more inland. It should not take us more than a dozen days to get out and back."

"I shall be looking for you, then," said Craig, "in a couple of weeks."

"That should be about right," Andy answered.

"How will Craig know when we are coming back to the rainforest?" the shaman asked Andy.

"Craig goes *jogging* on the grassland every morning," the god replied.

"What is *jogging*?"

"It is like running," Craig answered, "but it is not as fast as running."

"Not the way you do it," Andy said to Craig.

"Oh, but I am slowing down, in my old age."

"Old age," the shaman mimed. "How is it that you two never grow old?"

"It is Big Medicine," Andy answered.

"I know Big Medicine," said the shaman. "But I know of no Big Medicine that keeps a person young."

"It was not our doing," said Andy. "So, we cannot account for it."

"Was it the doing of the Glittering Gods?" the shaman inquired.

"The Glittering Gods?" Andy asked.

"Whenever I see these gods," said the shaman, "they are glittering. And they seem to have no constant form."

"We have never seen the Glittering Gods," said Craig. "But I have heard them talk. What do you know about the Glittering Gods?"

"Not as much as I would like to know," said the shaman. "I believe the Glittering Gods brought my tribe here. And they brought you here."

"This is what we also suppose," said Andy.

"Do the Glittering Gods ever talk to you?" Craig asked the shaman.

"I believe the Glittering Gods did talk to me once," the shaman replied. "But my memory of this occurrence is hazy. And ever since, I knew certain events would happen, long before they happened. I believe the Glittering Gods gave me a special gift."

"The gift of clairvoyance," Andy said.

"That clears up a few queries I've had," Craig muttered.

"The Tree Spirit talks to me, though."

"The Tree Spirit?" Andy inquired.

"I know who the Tree Spirit is," Craig said.

"Who is it?" Andy asked.

"A fellow named Creighton Beryl."

"But the sound of the Tree Spirit has changed," said the shaman.

"That would be the sound of Reginald Wylie," said Craig. "I call him Reg."

"Is Reg *the guy I know*?" Andy asked, in English.

"Yeah, he is. But, before Reg, *the guy I know* was Creighton."

"Are those two involved with the Glittering Gods?" Andy queried.

"Yeah," said Craig. "They are employed by the Glittering Gods, to keep tabs on us. And to help us out, if need be."

"Why is that?"

"Would you believe that we are a *reality show* on *television*?"

"What is *television*?" the shaman asked.

"What is a *reality show*?" Andy followed up.

"I can see I have some explaining to do." Craig poured the shaman a third cup of coffee. "Have another doughnut, you two. This will take a while."

30—THE RETURN OF THE SHAMAN

It required no coaxing from Craig to convince Koree to sign up for another tour of duty aboard the *Albatross II*. She took to the enterprise with a squeal of delight.

The successive morning, Koree and Craig were waiting at the bus stop when Andy's aircraft landed.

"Do you want to take the ship out?" Andy asked Koree.

The young woman made no verbal reply, but rushed to the bridge of the *Albatross II* and initiated the pre-flight checklist.

"That girl is an inveterate pilot," Craig said to Andy, in English.

"Amelia Earhart reborn," Andy answered.

"Just don't let her fly over the Pacific," Craig advised.

Andy snickered, but the shaman was bemused.

"Although I have come to know much of your *lingo*," said the medicine man, "I often have no idea what you two are talking about."

"Yeah," said Craig. "We should come with annotations."

"May the Force be with us," Andy chaffed.

The shaman shrugged. "The Force is always with us."

"True that," Andy replied.

And he signaled Koree to take off.

*****

Days later, Craig espied the *Albatross II* on the western horizon and loped to the bus stop.

The grinning shaman exited, escorted by a dejected Koree.

“Why are you so glum,” Craig asked the young woman.

“That was my final journey,” Koree replied, as she listlessly slapped his hand.

“Why are you so giddy?” Craig asked the shaman.

“That was my next-to-final journey,” the shaman replied. “And I saw wondrous things.”

“True that,” Koree replied, in English.

As the trio entered the rainforest, the shaman babbled on about the experiences he’d had and the marvels he’d seen.

“It was better than I dreamt,” the shaman summed up.

“You dreamt of the world outside the valley?” Craig queried.

“My apprentice calls them visions. But, if they were visions, they pale in comparison to the real thing.”

“Life is like that,” said Craig.

“We are in accord,” said the shaman.

*****

The medicine man sat against the trunk of a tree overlooking Brook Haven in the Forest.

Koree went to the creek to fetch the shaman some water, while Craig stayed with the oldster.

"You must be tired," Craig said.

"I am fatigued. But I have one more journey to make."

"What journey is that?"

"The journey to the undiscovered country," the shaman replied, in English, "from whose bourn no traveler returns."

The medicine man closed his eyes and ceased breathing.

Craig didn't know what to do.

He thought about performing cardiopulmonary resuscitation. But he was reminded of the last occasion he had administered CPR.

It had been a beloved family pet. And Craig successfully brought the dog back from the dead—only to have it expire again, an hour later. Craig saw this intercession as futile and doltish.

"To die once," he surmised, "ought to be enough. And to lie beneath a tree and take one last look at what you helped to create. And to see that it's a good thing. And to die in your sleep. That's a fine death. Better than most."

Craig surveyed the reposing shaman and inquired aloud: "But how in the world did that old fellow know *Hamlet*?"

*****

Aleesa and Dora ritually prepared the shaman's body—which was, hours later, buried in the Sacred Knoll.

Aleesa must have let the proverbial cat out of the bag, Craig deduced, since all of the women, even the youngest girls, were present for the ceremony—and the shaman was interred in close proximity to Zeena and her parents.

Ginger and Snap were also in attendance. And they were among the last to leave.

"What do you suspect those animals think about this business?" Craig asked his spouse.

"Perhaps," Dora replied, "they do not think at all. Perhaps they naturally accept the inevitable."

"Did Rance say that?"

"I said that. It is a good way to live."

"And it is a good way to die. But I firmly believe that animals feel grief as deeply and sharply as we do. They just keep it to themselves."

"Why do you say this?"

"In my youth, I saw a dead *raccoon* by the side of a road."

"What is a *raccoon*?"

"A small furry animal that wears a mask."

"Be serious," Dora insisted.

"I am being serious. But what I am trying to say is that the mate of the raccoon refused to leave its side, until the dead raccoon was removed."

"Who removed the dead raccoon?"

"A man whose job it was to do such things."

"Is there much call for this work?"

"I suspect there is, Dora. But what I am trying to say is that the raccoon stayed by its mate for more than a day."

"Perhaps the live raccoon did not know what to do."

"The live raccoon likely was a husband."

"Why do you say that?"

"Husbands require constant supervision and advice from their wives."

"We are in accord," Dora replied.

31—KOREE COMES OUT OF RETIREMENT AGAIN

Word came to Craig, via Rance's Rangers—who were making their monthly visit to Brook Haven in the Forest—that Andy wanted Koree to take over the commuter airline.

"But what about Vik and Sluggo?" Craig inquired.

"They're busy raising kids," Barney the Machinist replied.

"You mean Seth and Josh and Jon?"

"Darned right," said George the Blacksmith. "Those boys are a handful."

"But aren't the parents helping out?"

"The adults have other jobs to do," replied Phil the Butcher. "Earth Town depends on them, twenty-six/seven."

"Yeah, I can see that. But why are Vik and Sluggo shouldering most of the childcare burden?"

"That's the way it goes sometimes," Bailey the Carpenter replied.

"But, you know, Koree doesn't wear a T-shirt, ever."

"Nobody cares about that," Tim the Meat Cutter replied. "Not even Janis."

"Yeah, I can see that. Janis comes here often. But does she want her son to see a nearly naked female?"

"Why not?" Tim asked. "The younger boys are going to come to the rainforest eventually, right?"

"Yeah, I suspect they will."

"I don't think anybody has a problem with bare skin," said Phil.

"Yeah, it's just that habits and mores die hard."

"Right," said Barney. "But the old ways have to go. You've got to keep moving on, right?"

"Yeah, and it's a new world, with a new outlook on life."

"Copy that," said George.

"But what about Andy?"

"He's got other irons in the fire," George replied.

"Oh, yeah? What particular irons are those?"

"For one thing," said Bailey, "he's busy writing another book."

"About his travels," said Tim.

"Yeah, I should've realized that."

"To be more in line with the facts," said Tim, "it's a continuation of his original book."

"That thing must be huge now."

"It is," said Bailey. "Andy has it bound up in volumes. And the whole shebang fills up half a shelf in the library."

"He's been busy."

"And that's not all," said Tim. "When Andy is done with the book, he's going to chart the stars."

"You mean no one has done that, yet?"

"Vik and Sluggo made a stab at it," Phil replied, "with that telescope you got them. But Andy intends to finish the job."

"Do you think Andy will name any constellations after us?"

"Probably," said Barney. "The Butcher and the Baker and the Machinist and the Blacksmith and the Carpenter and the Electrician."

"Naw," said George, "I don't think that would be the way to do it. I think you have to name constellations after mythical heroes and animals and such."

"Andy is trying to scope out our solar system," said Bailey. "He says there are planets out there. And he thinks the disposition here might be a whole lot like Earth's solar system."

"He might be right," the electrician replied. "I'm interested in learning the outcome."

*****

So it was that Koree took charge of the commuter airline business. And she was the happiest Craig had ever seen her.

Whenever Koree was in Earth Town, during the first few weeks, she took up residence in Gloria's Quonset hut. And she did double-duty as the colony's seamstress.

Koree, who had learned how to sew from Gloria, even took to wearing a mithrill *Earthling* T-shirt she made for herself.

Since the *Albatross II* had to spend layovers at the edge of the rainforest, the males of Earth Town put up a hangar, with motorized retractable rollers, for it there.

Koree was now lodging in two municipalities. And she divided her attention almost equally between them.

*****

"I told you it was a good idea for Koree to go with Andy," Gloria happily refreshed Craig's memory. "Koree needed to confront her demons and find a purpose in life."

"Spoken like a true educator," Craig replied.

"High praise," Gloria remarked, "coming from my mentor."

"You seem to be the mentor now, my friend."

"The times are changing, aren't they?"

"Yeah, it's a brave new world. I never know what's going to happen next."

"Exciting, isn't it?"

"Yeah, but, you know, some things never change."

"Like death and taxes?"

"Yeah, but death didn't get worse, every time Congress convened."

"That's cogent, Craig."

"I paraphrased Will Rogers. I recently read a book about him."

"Which brings me to the fact that we need to put up a library here," said Gloria. "I've been storing the extra textbooks and sketches in my hut. And I'm running out of room."

"Can't we throw together another hut out of thatch and wicker?"

"No, we need something that will keep out the damp. I was thinking of concrete."

"Will Aleesa let us build a concrete library?"

"No, not here. We'd have to put it out by the medical facility and the showers."

"But that's an hour's slog from here."

"A half-hour," said Gloria, "when I jog."

"You're right. Some things have changed."

"Have you noticed that most everybody around here jogs, rather than just walking places?"

"Now that you mention it."

"It's because of you, Craig. The little girls took to copying you, years ago. And now they're adults. They walk on hunts and to the river for fishing. But, for most everything else, they jog around."

"Do you think that's a bad thing?"

"No, but it's different. It's another thing that's changing. Kids need paragons more than they need critics."

"You're a good teacher, my friend."

"And so are you, my friend," replied Gloria. "Together, I think we're making a difference."

32—GOLDEN AGE

Orv Elliot engendered the trend, in Earth Town's days of yore. Orv was a mason, so he was particularly busy when the Earthlings had a construction project in Earth Town or on the edge of the rainforest. Otherwise, he was mostly at his leisure.

One morning, Orv, who had been raised on a dairy farm, stopped by to help Linda and Chris milk the goats and antelope. He came back again for the late afternoon milking.

The attendant day, Richie the Plumber and Roy the Mechanic helped Mike the Horticulturalist with the gardens and orchards and vineyard.

Within a week, all of the men were engaged in agrarian pursuits of some kind. Even Dan the Dentist deigned to lend a hand. Linda and Chris and Mike welcomed the assistance and served as supervisors.

Koree, who was now ensconced in Gloria's Quonset hut, pitched in with agriculture and horticulture—when she wasn't flying the *Albatross II* or working at Gloria's sewing machines.

It became a way of life with the Earth Town occupants to volunteer for duties outside their professions. And everyone seemed to profit from this.

The veldt dwellers had perennially combined forces for the cereal harvest and housing projects and hunting and fishing expeditions. But now, they were helping each other out with cooking and baking and plumbing and carpentry and meat-cutting.

Craig was called in from the rainforest for electrician jobs, though. None of the other Earthlings felt comfortable dealing with electricity.

Whenever Craig was in Earth Town, he learned as much as he could from the men about their occupations—even to the extent of doing research on them in library books.

But education was not confined to Earth Town. Five girls in Brook Haven in the Forest formed a Medical Club. They were daily drilled in health care by Sheela. And they accompanied the sylvan physician on her rounds. The Medical Club received instruction from Doctor Johnson and Nancy the Nurse, whenever they visited the rainforest.

The plan was for the five of them to serve as Sheela's assistants—so that they, too, could become physicians. The adult versions of themselves would, in turn, train new members of the Medical Club, *ad infinitum.*

If cooperation was the watchword in this new world, so was compliance. Although no laws were "on the books," everyone in the women's parish and the pampas hamlet was a law-abiding citizen.

Linda Martinez had been a police chief on Earth. But, on this planet, she had become a dairy farmer and a mayor and a justice of the peace.

Linda had promulgated only one law—or ordinance, as she called it. This was that no alcohol, be it wine or beer or distilled liquor, was permitted on the plains. And the colonists, to her astonishment, unanimously favored this ordinance.

Linda had banned spirits, partly because Dan the Dentist was a recovering alcoholic, and partly because she knew that alcohol spells trouble—even among the best of people. And Linda was not about to brook any botheration in Earth Town.

In Brook Haven in the Forest, there were unwritten codes of conduct. And no one ever strayed from them.

The chieftain's decisions were sacrosanct. If there was any dissatisfaction with a dictate, the grumbling was low-key and of brief duration.

The same had become a fact of life in the fisher-folk enclave. The elders served as a rubber stamp for the chieftain's opinions.

No one questioned the actions of the new shaman, either. But this was mainly because Loda followed the traditions of the quondam medicine man and never varied from his predecessor's medical practices.

When the chieftain and elders occasionally consulted Loda on a vexing matter, the shaman immediately checked in with the Tree Spirit—who came through with canny counseling and unfailing prognostication.

*****

"If this is a Golden Age," Craig said to Rance, "I have one thing to say."

"What's that?" the hunter inquired.

"When is it all going to start falling apart? That's what happens with Golden Ages, you know. They ultimately lose their luster."

"The whole while I've known you, *amigo*, you've been a worried man."

"Yeah, I am a bit of a Nervous Nellie."

"I know there's such a thing as entropy. And order turns into chaos. You taught me that."

"Yeah, that's the second law of thermodynamics."

"And look, *amigo*, I realize the importance of being proactive and heading off trouble. And we've been doing that. And you know I'm a deliberate sort of guy. But there's also such a thing as savoring the good life, while you have it."

"Yeah, there's something in what you say."

"You're bugged about losing things. And I can savvy that. Life is loss. But, in the immortal words of Doctor Seuss: 'Don't be sad because it's over. Be happy that it happened.'"

"You've been in the library again, haven't you?"

"Reading is fundamental."

"True that."

"Let the future take care of itself, *amigo*. You can't control everything."

"Yeah," said Craig. "But a fellow can try, can't he?"

33—SARA GROWS

Even as a toddler, Sara was big for her age. And when she turned twelve, she was taller than all of the teenagers.

Sara could throw a spear harder than Dora. And her aim was nearly as accurate as her instructor's.

The same was true of Sara's prowess with a bow and arrow. Only Gloria could surpass her in this regard.

As a twelve-year-old, Sara ran with Craig in the early mornings and was the swiftest sprinter among the women. When she was sixteen, Sara could knock out nearly as many consecutive push-ups and pull-ups and chin-ups and dips as Craig could.

After a few lessons, Sara was easily the best swimmer among the females. On some mornings, she loped to the northern river and swam for an hour—and was back before sundown.

Sara had also been the brainiest student in Gloria's morning school. She owned an aptitude for learning language and was fluently bilingual by the age of six.

The two areas in which Sara did not excel were art and sewing. Koree and Gloria had done their best to teach Sara the rudiments of drawing and darning and stitching, but the girl showed a paucity of talent for these pursuits.

"It's because her hands are so big," Koree said to Gloria, in English. "Sara understands what to do. But she can't make her fingers follow her thoughts."

"That sums it up," the instructor replied.

"But even though Sara isn't good at art and sewing, she could teach art and sewing."

"I think you're right, Koree. Some of the best teachers were failures at everything else."

"Knowledge is better than talent. Is that what you're saying?"

"Yes, that's often true."

"Then, it would be good to learn how to do as many things as possible."

"Yes, it would."

"I should probably visit the library more often," said Koree.

"Yes," Gloria replied. "We all should."

*****

Although Sara didn't sleep in the same hut as Aleesa and Rance and Ginger and Snap, the girl spent most of her waking hours with them.

Sara was waiting, when Ginger and Snap stirred to wakefulness each morn, and was determined to be the one who fed them. Sara did this, not to purchase the loyalty of these animals, but out of love for them. Ginger and Snap equated Sara with provender and knew that she would provide them with the means to sate their hunger.

At the age of sixteen, in accordance with custom, a separate hut was furnished for Sara. And this hut became a recurrent gathering spot for girls and young women.

Aleesa had recognized Sara's leadership qualities, early on, and the chieftain did her best to train Sara to be her successor. In spite of this, Aleesa endeavored not to show favoritism toward Sara.

But Aleesa's sisters were not beguiled; nor did they envy Sara's exalted status. Sara had learned how to be a leader—without seeming to be bossy or make anyone jealous of her.

Aleesa never told Sara (or the other women) of Sara's parentage. And Aleesa swore Dora and Janis and Craig and Rance to secrecy, concerning this. Like her sisters, Sara knew nothing of her origins—and never wanted to be relieved of such ignorance.

In short, the indigenous constituents of Brook Haven in the Forest had been abandoned by their tribe. Henceforth, they wanted nothing to do with those who had deserted them.

This feeling extended even to the visitors who hid at the periphery. While studiously ignoring these interlopers, every female in the community seethed with resentment at the sight of them. It was only fealty to their chieftain which prevented them from lashing out against their on-looking relatives.

Sara especially despised the tourists. "If I were chieftain," she told Rance, when she was yet a child, "I would have them slain."

"If you were chieftain," Rance replied, "you would know better."

"Why would I know better?"

"Because a chieftain has to be a better person than that. And you have to be a better person than that, Sara. You were meant to be a better person than that."

This was a one-time conversation. But it was an exchange that Sara kept in mind for the rest of her life.

"I am meant to be a better person," she told herself. "Rance has said so. And therefore, it must be true. And thus, I shall work every day to become a better person."

Rance had no idea how salient and substantial his words had been to the youthful Sara. But he would never regret saying them.

"As the twig is bent," Rance, years later, recounted, "so grows the tree."

And, for Sara, this was so.

34—BOYS' LIFE

Seth and Josh and Jon looked up to Vik and Sluggo. And nothing the older boys said or did could diminish them in the hearts of the three younger boys.

Vik and Sluggo were able to pilot the *Albatross II* and had flown the great airship to another realm. Vik and Sluggo had seen fabulous and ferocious fauna. They had seen the habitation of the forestland females. And they had seen the stronghold of the fisher folk. These were places only dreamt of in the grandest fantasies of Seth and Josh and Jon.

To the preteen troika, Vik and Sluggo were what they desired to be—but never truly believed they could be. Vik and Sluggo were viewed as the finest and the smartest. They had done everything that was worth doing. And they were devoting their latter days to teaching what they knew.

Seth and Josh and Jon drank in every word spoken by Vik and Sluggo. And if Seth or Josh or Jon inferred that he had not met the expectations of Vik and Sluggo, the youth cried himself to sleep and yearned for a better tomorrow.

Seth and Josh and Jon unequivocally loved their parents. But there is something about an older boy that rivets the attention and admiration of a lesser lad. Vik and Sluggo were bigger than life, yet they never acted that way. And this, too, made a difference.

Vik and Sluggo had never been students in a quintessential pedagogical setting, but they adopted this educational format for the tutelage of Seth and Josh and Jon. The library became a makeshift schoolhouse. And Vik and Sluggo took turns as the schoolmaster.

The younger boys learned at their own paces, though. And nothing was foisted upon them, save the memorization of arithmetic tables.

Like their heroic gurus, Seth and Josh and Jon had a thirst for knowledge. No subject was too dull; no topic too abstruse.

*****

Although the five lads listened to classical music compact discs, they didn't have any musical instruments to play. Janis, who had taken six years of piano lessons, once asked if any of the boys wanted to learn how to "tickle the ivories."

"Where would we get a piano?" Vik inquired.

"Mister Harrison could probably provide one," the physician touted.

"But to what advantage?" Vik asked. "None of us would ever be as good as the musicians on the CDs, even if we practiced for hours, every day."

"That's likely true," Janis answered. "But it's not germane. Playing the piano is fun."

"I'm afraid we don't have time for piano playing now," said Sluggo. "We have to concentrate on math and science. Maybe we can do piano later."

"But there's not always a *later*," the physician remonstrated. "None of us is promised tomorrow."

"I can't argue with that logic," said Sluggo.

"We'll seriously mull over the matter," said Vik.

"In the meanwhile," said Janis, "I'll see if Mister Harrison can scare us up a keyboard or two. I miss playing."

"It wouldn't hurt to have one or two keyboards around," Vik acceded.

"And maybe some other stringed instruments, too," said Sluggo.

"I'll see what Mister Harrison can do," said Janis.

"I don't expect there's anything he can't do," said Vik.

"Yes," said Janis. "That man is a treasure. A true treasure. I don't know what we would've done without him, all these years."

*****

A few days later, the boys discovered an upright digital piano in the library—and apprised Doctor Johnson.

"This is excellent," the physician said. "There are no strings in a digital piano, so no tuning is necessary. And, of course, replacing broken strings isn't an issue. And a digital piano has pedals, like a traditional piano. And the keys are weighted, to feel like a traditional piano. And yet, a digital piano isn't as heavy as a traditional upright."

"And it's electronic," Vik replied. "You just plug it in."

"Where did Mister Harrison get it?" Sluggo queried.

"And how did he get it into the library?" Vik tagged on.

"I make it a policy not to ask," Janis answered.

*****

Vik and Sluggo got the ball rolling by taking piano lessons from Doctor Johnson. When Seth and Josh and Jon found out, they insisted on enrolling in classes, too.

Before long, most of the Earth Town populace was studying piano and had portable electronic keyboards in their Quonset huts for home practice.

And when word reached Brook Haven in the Forest, Sara nagged Craig to set her up with a digital piano, as well. Craig, who had taken piano lessons in his youth, taught the woodland girls the basics. And he obtained portable keyboards, connected to solar panels, for them to practice on. Doctor Johnson provided advanced training during her sylvan visits.

Within a year, recitals were being held in both provinces. Sara, ever the competitor, insisted on a contest with the prairie pianists.

The boys flew to Brook Haven in the Forest for the euphonic showdown. Sara claimed that the girls were more musically adept than the boys. But Janis diplomatically declared the Battle of the Keyboardists (which became an annual affair) a draw.

*****

Ginger and Snap disapproved of this piano playing, however. They slunk away at the first plink of a key—be it black, white, sharp, natural, or flat.

"I reckon there's something in the sounds of a musical instrument that dogs and cats don't appreciate," Rance said to Craig.

"You might be on to something there," the electrician replied.

"I wasn't partial to the piano on Earth," said Rance. "But I don't mind hearing the eighty-eights being twiddled here in the wild. And I get a kick out of listening to the classical music CDs. It's like the sounds of civilization followed us."

"I can see where this is going," Craig said. "The girls will be hitting me up next for other musical instruments. And we'll end up with a girls' band."

"That sounds like trouble," replied Rance, "with a capital T."

"Yeah," said Craig. "Right here in River City."

35—GOOD SPORTS

It all started when Vik and Sluggo elected to show Seth and Josh and Jon how to play chess. They found a book on the Game of Kings and Queens in the library and got a few tips from Andy Cooper, who had been a club champion in his youth. It wasn't long before a town-wide tournament was inaugurated—and it became an annual event.

In order for this to happen, though, Bailey the Carpenter had to consult with the females of Brook Haven in the Forest on the manufacture of chess boards and the carving of chess pieces—and another cottage industry was born.

*****

When Vik and Sluggo stumbled upon a manual on how to play kickball, they hit up Andy Cooper again. The deity huddled with the other adults in Earth Town, and a kickball diamond-in-the-rough sprang into being—courtesy of sacks of grass seed and a brace of solar-powered riding lawn mowers from Craig's surreptitious purveyor. The electrician also came through with the necessary accoutrements of the game: Balls and bases and a backstop.

The subsequent sport to be taken up was soccer. Again, it was the boys who started things off, but it was the grown-ups who joined in for fun. By and by, it was necessary to put in a soccer pitch—contiguous to the kickball outfield.

*****

When word of this reached Brook Haven in the Forest, Sara assembled a kickball team, a soccer roster, and a chess squad. The men of Earth Town laid out a diamond and a pitch near the woodland medical facility.

Within a year, monthly games were being played between Earth Town and Brook Haven in the Forest—contestants and spectators being shuttled to and fro by the *Albatross II*.

Ginger and Snap were persistently on hand when the bouts were held near the jungle. The animals sat on their haunches and watched with mild interest. But they never moved from their positions or made a sound. When the athletic activity was terminated, the dog and cat re-entered the rainforest.

"What do Ginger and Snap make of all this?" Rance inquired of his wife, in English.

"They probably long ago came to the conclusion that humans are stark-raving mad," Aleesa answered. "And this is yet further proof to buttress their belief."

"Stark-raving mad? Buttress their belief? Who taught you to talk like that?"

"Dora. She picks up Earth Town talk from Craig."

"And she reads library books, too."

"True that," the chieftain replied.

*****

Kickball games and soccer matches were friendly scrimmages—which lasted for hours. Everyone, who wanted to play, got to play. And scores were never kept.

"Who needs to win or lose?" Andy Cooper put forth. "It's all about having fun, isn't it? At least, that's the way it was for me, when I was a kid."

No one, except Sara, took issue with this non-contentious philosophy.

Chess was another matter, however. And, for this reason, Vik and Sluggo never competed with anyone. They were content to coach.

"Why would I want to pit myself against an opponent?" Vik mooted. "I can work on chess problems in the books for myself. That's more interesting, anyway. And there are no timing clocks or hard feelings involved."

Sluggo fervently embraced this perspective.

Craig and Rance and Andy also stayed out of the fray.

The hunter spoke for all three when he said: "We had our fill of competition on Earth."

*****

Another exception was track-and-field. Sara got together with Vik and Sluggo to set up meets between the boys and girls.

All of the footraces, up to a quarter-mile, were held on a straight-away, point-to-point. The half-mile was forth-and-back. The mile was forth-and-back twice.

Field events included the shot-put and discus, throwing a spear (for distance and accuracy), and archery. The boys came in second on accuracy. And Sara could hurl a javelin farther than anyone.

Since the girls outnumbered the boys, they compiled more points than the boys did in track-and-field events. The redoubtable Sara was unbeatable at any distance.

But Vik and Sluggo and Seth and Josh and Jon didn't mind a bit. Each engagement was an opportunity to mingle with juveniles of the opposite sex.

And it was for this latter reason that all co-ed track-and-field meets and kickball games and soccer matches and chess tournaments were assiduously monitored by adults at both venues.

"Look, but don't touch," Nancy and Linda and Janis mandated. "Talk, but keep it G-rated."

The same restrictions, couched in the Woodlander language, were expressed by Aleesa and Dora and Gloria.

But the boys and girls found ways to secretly convene. And a few romances resulted.

"As long as it's strictly *puppy love*," the Earth Town mothers concurred. "But no teenage wedlock. Not for our boys."

"When would be a good time for the boys to get married?" Dan asked his spouse.

"Maybe when they're in their forties or fifties," Linda answered.

And she meant it.

36—LODA TAKES CHARGE

The fisher-folk enclave was all abuzz about the departure of the shaman, as reported to them by Paul.

"What do you mean, My Chieftain," inquired Borg, the youngest elder, "when you say that the shaman melted into the morning mists?"

"Primarily that, Borg."

"And this is all that the shaman said?"

"There was more, Borg. But it was of a personal nature."

"My Chieftain, what will we do without the shaman?"

"We have Loda."

"Do you believe Loda is up to the job?"

"When you think about it," Paul replied, "Loda has been doing most of the shaman's work, for lo these many cycles of the stars."

"While this is true, My Chieftain, we always had the shaman here, lest Loda made a mistake."

"But Loda never made a mistake."

Borg grunted. "Yet, My Chieftain, it will not be the same."

"We are in accord, Borg. But what choice do we have?"

"We can search for the shaman."

"When the shaman said goodbye, Borg, he meant *goodbye forever*. Even if the shaman has not died, he has likely gone to another place, far from here, where we would never be able find him."

"Then, My Chieftain, you think the shaman has not died?"

"I do not believe the shaman could ever truly die, Borg."

"Do you think the shaman is flying with the God in the Sky?"

"It would not surprise me," the chieftain replied.

*****

If Borg was uncertain of Loda's abilities, Loda was even more so. And, yet, the new shaman plunged into his duties, knowing full well that everything he said and did would be open to scrutiny and suspicion.

But Loda had learned well from his predecessor. He knew all of the healing arts.

Loda also understood the importance of listening. He spoke only when it was necessary to do so. And, by and by, every villager came to construe his laconic conduct as competence and wisdom.

Whenever Loda did need help, he called upon the Tree Spirit or conferred with Rance and Craig, when they met at the Halfway Mark (a clearing between the parishes) for the weekly trade-and-talk.

If the novice shaman ever forgot something he'd been taught by his master, Loda prevailed upon Craig to read to him an applicable section from the book which the God in the Sky had written—wherein much of the fisher-folk medical information had been set down. Craig regularly carried an indexed hand-copied lore-chapter of this literature with him on the trade-and-talk parlays.

Since it was the shaman's duty to select the next chieftain, Loda kept his eyes and ears open for likely candidates. The front-runner was Borg's eldest son, Tohbee.

As a teenager, Tohbee had already grown taller and broader than Borg. And he was the best hunter and fisherman in the stronghold. The boy had a brain in his head, too.

Tohbee would have served as an excellent apprentice for Loda. But Tohbee was destined to tread another path: He would be a worthy successor to Paul.

With Tohbee out of the running, Loda had been captivated by a teenager of lofty intelligence. The problem was that this candidate was a female, by the name of Lin. And there had never been, in anyone's memory, a distaff shaman.

When Loda approached Paul about making Lin his apprentice, the chieftain meditated a moment prior to answering. "I know Lin well. She is a shrewd young lady. She would make a fine shaman someday."

Loda tried not to act as astounded as he felt. "Will you ask her parents, then, for their approval?"

"Is that my job?"

"According to the precepts of our forefathers," Loda replied, "it is the chieftain's chore to prevail upon the parents."

"Then, Loda, I shall do so."

*****

Lin was thrilled to have been chosen as Loda's apprentice, but her parents were leery. It helped a great deal, though, that Paul had endorsed Loda's decision. And so it was that Lin reported to Loda's hut, early in the morning.

"There is much for you to learn, Lin," Loda exhorted her. "And may the God in the Sky grant me enough time to teach you."

"What shall we do today, Master?"

Loda was inwardly amused and charmed by Lin's use of the word *Master* to denominate him. But he attempted not to let this be apparent.

"Today, Lin, we shall go to the Halfway Mark for the trade-and-talk. There, you will meet someone you must get to know well, for he has much knowledge."

"Do you speak of the Tree Spirit, Master?"

"I speak of Craig," Loda replied.

"The angel of the God in the Sky?"

"The very same. And someday, Lin, you will have an opportunity to meet the God in the Sky."

"I am afraid of heights, Master."

"I think you will find the God in the Sky to be down-to-earth, Lin."

"What of the Tree Spirit, Master?"

"You will find the Tree Spirit down-to-earth, too, Lin."

*****

From that day forward, Lin and Loda went to the trade-and-talk parleys to converse with Craig and Rance (the angels of the God in the Sky).

Lin listened carefully whenever Craig read from *The Book of the Sky God.*

Those things Lin heard, which she didn't understand, she had Loda elucidate for her on the way home.

"What I am unable to teach you," the shaman said, early on, "is how to listen to what the wind is saying and to envision what the stars are revealing. There is also the discernment of the jewels." Loda rattled his leather pouch of precious gems. "These are things you must learn on your own."

"Who is to guide me, Master?"

"I shall tell you what my master told me, when I asked him the same question: 'Listen to your heart. And keep your mind open.'"

"I fear that these are labors beyond my abilities, Master."

"Be of good cheer, Lin. All will be revealed to you, if you are patient."

"Patience is something I must also learn, Master."

"If you have wisdom, Lin, patience will follow. Everything follows from wisdom."

"Everything, Master?"

"Everything good, Lin."

"Then, Master, I shall be patient and good."

"I could not ask for more," replied Loda.

37—TOURISM

For decades, groups of females from the fisher-folk enclave had periodically made presumably clandestine visits to Brook Haven in the Forest—hearkening to a time when the borough had been called Zeena's village.

These mothers and sisters and nieces and cousins and grandmothers of the abandoned infants had witnessed glorious things.

They had seen the God of the Bearded Countenance (now known as the God in the Sky) walking and talking with their castoffs—and knowing that the deity would never walk and talk with them, inasmuch as they were not worthy.

They had seen the deity's companion: A marvelous golden four-legged creature, which could see them when others could not, yet did not betray their presence.

They had seen the creature's companion: A black panther, like the vicious felines they had once hunted and killed. This cat also could see them, yet did not drive them away.

The visitors smelled the delicious aroma of baking bread and grieved that they could not make such food for themselves—but had to trade salt for day-old baked goods.

They saw and smelled the variety of unidentifiable fruits and vegetables and nuts and legumes and other edibles brought from the grassland settlement. Such luxuries were denied them.

They heard classical music being played on solar-powered compact disc machines.

They saw and heard musical instruments wielded by the younger females, who attended school each morning in a thatched open-air pavilion.

The fisher-folk women had no experience with music and, at first, could not take it all in. But they had come to adore it.

Nor did they comprehend the utility of learning impractical sciences. But they were enthralled to hear the seamstress/teacher, called Gloria, speak of matters beyond their cognizance.

They gloried at the children who scratched cryptic markings with white tubes upon black slates. And these incomprehensible symbols were somehow translated into recognizable speech.

They were thunderstruck by the way the children depicted scenes of three dimensions onto a two-dimensional strip of bark called “paper.”

They saw Gloria teaching the girls to do something called “sewing” with mystifying machinery—and pondered its significance.

They saw the pale-skinned men and boys of the grassland—who came to visit the pale-skinned females of the woodland—and were benighted by their presence.

They saw the games, played by the boys and girls on the grassland at the border of the rainforest—and were awed.

Everything which the fisher-folk females saw and heard and smelled in this special world strengthened their belief that the place was a paradise—and the abandoned infants were fortunate to be living there.

"How blessed I am," the fisher-folk mothers mused, "to have given birth to someone who can reside in such splendor."

The fisher-folk women would've been shocked to discover that the inhabitants of this heavenly domain despised their mothers and sisters and nieces and cousins and grandmothers for discarding them, on account of their skin being a lighter shade. And they damned their relatives to a hellish demise for their discrimination.

But such messages were never transmitted. And the tourists from the fisher-folk stronghold invariably went back to their humdrum lives and cursed the day-old bread and went without surety of a better tomorrow.

38—FATHERHOOD

Seth and Josh and Jon had long been bugging Vik and Sluggo to take them fishing. The three youngsters had never seen a river or a mountain, except in library picture books, and they were champing at the bit to go.

Finally, Nancy and Linda and Janis granted their collective permission—on the proviso that adult male supervision would be present, and the three youngest would be taught to swim.

Since there was a maximum of six igloo-shaped collapsible tents in storage (they were used for fishing and hunting jaunts), it would not be possible for more than one chaperone to accompany the five youths. And the mothers of the minors came to the decision that this supervisor would be Dan the Dentist.

Dan, who had logged a multitude of hours with the boys in the library, was no outdoorsman and adamantly refused the nomination.

"But you're the one man we can spare right now," Chris the Farmer exposited. "Everyone else is too busy."

"What about Rance or Craig?" Dan importuned. "Hiking and camping and fishing are their long suits."

"But they don't live in Earth Town," Linda replied. "And it's Berry Picking Season in the jungle. They can't be spared."

"Berry Picking Season?" Dan groused. "Isn't it always Berry Picking Season over there?"

"No," Janis answered. "It just seems that way. It's like PBS pledge drives."

"But it's been ages since I swam," Dan quibbled. "And I don't know a fig about fishing."

"Don't give it another thought," said Linda. "Victor and David learned how to fish from Rance. And they took swimming lessons from Craig. They'll do all the work that needs to be done."

"Then, why do you require my presence?"

"In the event that something goes wrong," said Janis. "And you know darned well that something always goes wrong."

"You're not helping your argument any," Dan replied.

"Honey," said Nancy, "you're our insurance policy. With you there, we won't fret so much."

A sigh like a prayer fell from Dan's lips. "When do they want to go?"

"Not for another week," said Janis. "And that will give you an opportunity to prepare."

"Prepare," Dan reverberated. "Prepare for what?"

"The northern river is a full-day's hike from here," Janis answered. "You'll need to get your legs into shape."

"How am I going to do that?"

"You'll have to walk a lot every day," said Linda.

"Under a physician's guidance, of course," said Janis. "You don't want to overdo it and get blisters or cramps."

"But where would I do all this walking?"

"You could go back-and-forth on the quarter-mile track," said Linda. "That way, you'd be close to home if you got injured."

"Injured?"

"No one is saying you'll get injured," said Janis. "And you won't get injured, if you follow my instructions." The physician held up a sheet of paper. "I formulated a regimen."

The dentist assessed the proffered sheet. "On the second-to-the-last day," he bemoaned, "you've got me going thirty miles."

"The distance between here and the northern river is about forty miles," said Janis.

"Forty miles?" Dan yowled.

"But there's a silver lining," said Janis. "The last day of your training is an easy one. It's ten miles."

"That's an easy one?"

"And keep in mind that these days are broken up into increments," said Janis. "For example, on Day Six, you're going five miles before breakfast, five miles after breakfast, five miles before lunch, five miles after lunch—"

"Yes, yes, I get the picture. And it's not a pretty one. But tell me, can those boys really cover forty miles in a day? Seth and Josh and Jon are still kids."

"Well," said Janis, "let's be charitable and say that it will take your whole group two days to make it forty miles. That's twenty miles, maybe thirty miles, on the first day. You have to be ready for that."

"At least I can rest up, while they're fishing and swimming."

"You can get off your feet," said Linda. "But you'll have to watch those boys like a hawk. There are five of them. And one of you."

"Couldn't you give me two weeks to work up to that mileage?"

"I'm all for it," said Janis, "if the boys are. But I don't presume they can wait for more than one week, do you?"

Dan heaved another sigh. "No."

"All right then," said Janis. "Your training begins tomorrow, with a three-mile segment before breakfast."

Dan shook his head and gave Nancy the stink-eye. "This isn't what I signed on for, sweet-pea."

"That's fatherhood for you," his wife replied. "And let me tell you, honey-bun: Fatherhood is easier than motherhood."

"By a long shot," Linda ratified.

*****

Doctor Johnson made certain that Dan had clean socks and petroleum jelly and medical tape for his promenades.

"Why do I need the Vaseline?" the dentist wanted to know.

"You smear it on your toes," said Janis, "and under your arms and between your thighs. It prevents chafing and blisters."

"What's the tape for?"

"You wrap that around your toes and on the back of your heels, to prevent blisters. And you put the tape on, before you apply the petroleum jelly."

"Why do I have to wear a backpack?"

"Because you'll be wearing a backpack on your river ramblings," said Janis. "And the backpack will be full of food and water and equipment and a tent. You'll need to simulate game-day conditions. If you don't, you'll be sorry later."

"I'm sorry already."

"Now, now," cooed Janis. "That's no attitude to take. Keep in mind that you're doing this for the boys."

"What you're really saying is that I'm taking a hit for the team."

"Words to that effect, yes."

"I'd equally be willing for a dentist to be drilling."

"I know, Dan. But you'll thank me later. Make sure to drink water, every ten or fifteen minutes. And don't forget about electrolyte replacement."

"It's not that hot."

"Trust me, Dan. I'm an M.D. And I used to run half-marathons. I know about these things."

"Yes, ma'am."

"And take a break whenever you need one. This is practice. It's not the real deal, yet."

*****

The dentist followed his physician's peripatetic instructions to the letter. And, although Dan developed a few aches and pains, amid the ensuing week, he avoided blistering and dehydration.

By the morning of the first day of the riparian campaign, he was tanned, rested, and ready.

The younger boys didn't want to keep to the pokey tempo Dan set, so they dashed ahead.

"Stay close," Sluggo called after the threesome.

"Let them go," Vik said to Dan. "We'll reel them in later. They'll be tired and thirsty and want a rest."

"That's right," said Dan. "You fellows have been here before."

"And learned our lesson," said Sluggo. "Those guys will catch on soon enough, too."

And they did. By the afternoon, Seth and Josh and Jon kept to Dan's pace—and rested when he did. Shortly before sunset, according to Vik's estimation, the six of them had covered nearly thirty miles.

Vik showed Dan his compass. "The main thing is that we're walking in a straight line, or as straight as we possibly can. It's the shortest distance between two points."

"So I've heard," Dan replied.

"We should make camp before the sun goes down," Sluggo said.

"Where is a good spot?" Dan asked.

"Anywhere will do," Sluggo replied. "We're on level land. And there's no water about."

"Sensible considerations," said Dan.

The six of them laid down their backpacks, then and there, and set up their tents.

"No need for a fire," said Vik. "We'll have plenty of moonlight. There aren't any predators about. And we're not cooking a meal."

Dan examined the contents of his food pack. "Seeds and nuts and dried fruit and jerky," he itemized. "This is not my idea of *haute cuisine*."

"Tomorrow," said Sluggo, "we'll be frying fish."

"Okay," Dan admitted. "That's something to look forward to."

*****

The intrepid trekkers distinguished the peaks of mountains by midmorning and reached the northern river by noon of the second day. They made camp again, prior to breaking out the hooks and bobbers and bait (a mixture of cornmeal and vegetable oil in molded and hardened gobs), which tilapia (the sole fish species here) found irresistible.

The boys angled for a few hours—while enchanted by the foothills and mountain range facing them—before Dan announced that it was time for swimming lessons.

The stream was wide at this location, so the current was slow, and the water was warm. Also, the river bed was four feet deep, at its lowest level.

Just the same, Dan insisted that the boys stay close to shore. And he paid constant attention to them. When Seth and Josh and Jon had mastered the dog paddle, the dentist ordered them out of the water.

"Let's fry fish," Dan put forward.

This motion met with unanimous consent.

The boys took their catch on stringers from the river and brought them to the campfire which Vik and Sluggo had already arranged.

"Now that's what I call *haute cuisine*," a postprandial Dan espoused. "I could get used to this."

"I expect you want to head back tomorrow," said Sluggo.

"Not necessarily," said Dan, massaging a bare foot. "I should probably rest my dogs another day, if you don't mind."

The faces of the others were wreathed in smiles.

"You don't expect Mom will mind," Jon inquired.

"No, she'll be okay."

Dan neglected to mention that the objective was to spend at least two days fishing and swimming.

"You're the best," Jon said to his father.

"Okay," Dan decided. "That just made everything worth it."

39—HARVEST HOME

They called it Berry Picking Season in the woodlander language. But the category was broader.

For one thing, not all berries in the rainforest ripened simultaneously. But numerous varieties did. Accordingly, everyone in both woodlander municipalities went out to gather them.

And it wasn't just berries they were seeking. This was also an opportunity to collect herbs and spices, used for medical and cooking purposes.

Since the jungle communities were a day's march from each other, there was rarely an overlap of territories. Brook Haven in the Forest residents didn't typically encounter fisher folk during Berry Picking Season.

Because of divinable weather and rainfall patterns, three weeks after Berry Picking Season in the rainforest, it was Harvest Time on the savanna. In earlier years, the plains people had gathered endemic grasses to make their bread.

Since then, other strains of grain had been planted on the veldt, together with orchards of nut-bearing and fruit-bearing trees, and vast gardens of vegetables and fruit and herbs and spices, as well as vineyards of table grapes.

The plucking and uprooting occurred, and lasted for weeks, in advance of the cereal reaping. And every Earth Town occupant took part.

The six fishermen made it home, well before the tree-and-bush-and-garden gleaning commenced. And, shortly thereafter, they were joined by Koree and Dora and Craig and Rance.

In the days to come, the plains people and their friends dug up and grabbled at walnuts, almonds, peanuts, filberts, pistachios, cashews, hazelnuts, Brazil nuts, apples, apricots, pears, peaches, grapes, oranges, grapefruit, lemons, tomatoes, potatoes, carrots, lettuce, blackberries, blueberries, raspberries, strawberries—in addition to cacao and coffee (which grew in the shade of the orchards)—prior to tackling oats, barley, rye, and the indigenous wheat.

Cereal harvesting was done the old-fashioned way, with scythes and flails and a winnowing fan.

The initiatory grain cutting, decades before, had been a brutal affair—spurred by the risk of starvation, not to mention the threat of imminent attack from the fisher folk.

In later years, though, Harvest Time had become more laidback. Hard work and long hours were still involved. But fear was no longer a factor. It was a period of camaraderie and joy.

The prairie produce was steadily plentiful, insomuch as the soil was fertile and the weather was clement.

And it helped that Earth Town had two solar-powered dune buggies and two wagons to aid in the transfer of fruits and vegetables and herbs and nuts and grains to refrigerated storehouses.

"You know," Craig said to Rance, as they were grazing among blueberry bushes, "on Earth, these crops would be ripe in different months."

"Affirmative, *amigo*. There is something magical about this place."

"I don't believe in magic."

"I didn't believe in taxes, either. But I paid them."

"A compelling argument."

"It could be it's like what Arthur C. Clarke wrote," said Rance, "that magic is advanced technology we don't yet savvy."

"Yeah, maybe. But things here don't make a whole lot of sense, when you take a long, hard look at them."

"Okay, *amigo*. But you have to admit that it's sort of nice having everyone together, once a year. And we have a party, when we're all done. Except that when we're all done, we're too pooped to pant, much less party."

"Yeah, that is nice. And that is magical."

"And there's no telling when the magic will cease."

"Yeah, I get what you're saying, my friend. We should appreciate the good things, while we have them, and not take our blessings for granted."

"Affirmative, *amigo*. Because life is change. And things can change fast. And the changes aren't always to our liking."

Craig charily regarded his blueberry buddy. “That sounds ominous. Do you know something I don’t?”

“Negative, *amigo*. It’s nothing like that. It’s that I don’t see anything as being permanent.”

“Yeah, it’s a sober way to look at life.”

“And it’s a way to survive. You have to keep your eyes peeled. And when things are going well, and they keep going well, that’s when you need to watch out.”

“Yeah, I feel the same way. They call it being a pessimist.”

“Negative, *amigo*. That’s being a realist. And if we’re not realists, we’ll be in a heap of hurt.”

“Yeah, the ancient Greeks had a saying: ‘Don’t call a man fortunate, until he is dead.’”

“What does that mean?”

“Don’t jinx anyone. And that includes yourself.”

“Affirmative, *amigo*. I’m down with that.”

40—NINTH LIFE

Aleesa and Rance awoke to Ginger's whining. The dog was nudging the inert body of Snap. Even before touching the cold corpse of the elbastak, both Aleesa and Rance recognized death. Being hunters, they had seen it often.

"As big cats go," Rance would later tell Craig, "Snap lived a long life: Almost two decades."

Rance studied the white hairs on the elbastak's muzzle. They had cropped up more than a year ago—when Snap began to slow down. Ginger sensed that her companion could no longer keep up with her loping gait, and the canine had made allowances.

Rance cradled Snap's inanimate form and headed toward the Sacred Knoll, with Aleesa at his side and Ginger at their heels.

"Snap deserves to be buried there," Aleesa said.

"It seems right," Rance replied. "Snap was one of us."

Ginger watched while Aleesa and Rance excavated a grave. After the cat was interred and rocks piled atop a dirt mound, the dog remained at the Sacred Knoll.

"Ginger will probably be there for days," Aleesa said to Rance, in the woodlander tongue. "She stayed a long while, after Zeena was buried."

"I do not care what the experts say," Aleesa's husband replied. "Dogs do have feelings. They do feel grief. As much as humans do."

"I shall have to bring food and water to Ginger," said Aleesa. "That is what we had to do, when Zeena died."

"What made Ginger finally leave the Sacred Knoll?"

"I went to her and convinced her to come with me. It took some talking, though. I told her I needed her."

"Do you think that will work now?"

"I do not know. Ginger and Snap were together for many cycles of the stars."

"We'll need something to sweeten the pot," Rance said, in English.

"Do you have an idea?"

"I do," said Rance. "But I'll need to run it past Craig first."

*****

Thus it was that, three days later, a golden-brown, short-haired mongrel puppy, recently weaned, was introduced to a grieving Ginger at the Sacred Knoll.

The adult canine had just enough energy to lick the pup, which licked Ginger's muzzle in return.

Craig laid a bowl of shredded venison and another bowl of water in front of Ginger. The dog eagerly ate and drank, then directed her attention to the young one.

“That might have done the trick,” said Rance.

“Should we leave them alone?” Craig asked.

“I don’t reckon Ginger has enough strength to get back home by herself.”

“I’ll carry Ginger,” Craig proposed, “if you carry the pup.”

“Sold,” said Rance. “What should we call the little one?”

“Beats me. Any ideas?”

“How about Junior?”

“Junior sounds good to me.”

“Junior it is, then.”

“Life goes on,” Craig said, as he lifted Ginger.

“Affirmative,” replied Rance, lifting the pup.

“I’m going to miss Snap, though.”

“Snap was a good cat.”

“And a good friend.”

“Do you reckon there’s an Afterlife for animals?”

“If there is, I pray Snap finds good friends there.”

“Good friends,” said Rance. “That’s my idea of heaven.”

“Yeah, it often takes folks a lifetime to realize that.”

"And some never do."

"I once explained to Dora why Snap was being kept as a pet."

"These damsels never had a pet before Ginger, did they?"

"Not unless you count the goats they milk. But the women never even bothered to name the goats. I think Ginger was their first real experience with having a pet."

"What did you tell Dora?"

"I told her that animals were better than people."

"How so?"

"Animals, for the most part, express gratitude; whereas people, for the most part, don't."

"You'll get no argument from me on that."

"Animals, for the most part, stick by you; whereas people, for the most part, don't."

"Again, no argument."

"But Dora didn't get what I was saying, because her sisters consistently express gratitude. And they stick by one another. So, I told Dora that this is the way people were on Earth. What I call *my bygone world.* They often didn't feel grateful. And you couldn't count on them to stick by you."

"What did Dora say?"

"She said my bygone world must've been a horrible place. And, after I thought about it for a little while, I had to agree with her."

"Affirmative, *amigo*. This is definitely the better of our two worlds."

"With apologies to Voltaire, it might be the best of all possible worlds."

41—THE SEER SEES

Loda had yet learned nothing from the wind, no matter how hard he listened. Nor had he derived any message from the stars. But he had higher aspirations for the gems in his leather pouch.

Loda's master had claimed he didn't know how long ago the jewels had come into the possession of the fisher folk. No one could even say how ancient these uncut stones were.

Loda firmly believed the priceless pebbles had power, though. And he kept trying to find foreknowledge in them.

Loda's master had shown him that the stones must be dropped from the bag, in a certain manner and from a prescribed height, onto a leather skin—and where the jewels came to rest would show a pattern for the future.

It was not that Loda doubted his master. He had seen all of the medicine man's forecasts come to fruition. But Loda doubted his own ability to decode the gems.

For the umpteenth time, Loda watched the jewels bounce off the leather skin and establish a formation.

For the umpteenth time, Loda stared at the stones.

He called to memory his master's recommendation: "Empty your mind, Loda."

"That is an easy thing to say," Loda speculated. "But not an easy thing to do."

For the umpteenth time, he strove to empty his mind.

The fledgling shaman thought he might have fallen asleep, or at least slipped into a trance, because the configuration of the pebbles seemed to be making sense to him.

Moving images swam before Loda's eyes. He strained to see them better. He strained so hard and for so long that his head ached. But he didn't let the pain deter him from his mission.

And finally, the pain subsided.

He heard Lin call to him from outside his hut.

"That is strange," Loda cogitated. "Why would Lin be awake at this hour?"

Loda saw daylight streaming through cracks in the fur-flap doorway.

"How can the sun be up in the midst of night?" he asked himself.

He heard Lin call to him again.

"Come in," Loda answered.

The apprentice pushed up the pelt and ducked inside the hut to find the shaman with the gems spread before him—and she noted Loda's stricken expression.

"What did you see, Master?" Lin asked.

"I saw disturbing portents," Loda answered. "Yet, the stones never lie. The presentiment must be about to occur. Tell me, Lin, is today the day of the trade-and-talk at the Halfway Mark?"

"Today is the day, Master."

"Then, Lin, we must speak with the angels of the god. They will know what to do."

42—THE PARCEL

Lin and Loda detained Rance and Craig, once the trade-and-talk was completed and the fisher-folk representatives had departed with their beloved bread loaves in hand.

"Can you be here at the Halfway Mark in three days?" Loda inquired of the angels of the god, in English.

"I can clear my schedule," said Craig.

"Count me in, too," said Rance.

"Fine," said Loda. "Meet us here when the sun is directly overhead. And this is what you will need to bring with you."

*****

Three days later, Rance and Craig found Loda and Lin at the Halfway Mark at the appointed time.

"Here is the parcel of which we spoke," Loda said, in English.

"How did you know?" Rance asked.

"The stones told him," Lin replied.

"You mean Mick and the Boys?" Rance ingenuously queried.

Craig chortled. "I'll elaborate later about the stones," he said to Rance.

"What can be done?" Loda inquired.

"We have a plan," said Craig.

"This will keep happening," Loda said.

"How do you know?" Rance asked.

"The stones never lie," Lin answered.

*****

Koree met Craig at the border of the rainforest.

"I need a ride," Craig said.

"So I heard," Koree replied. "I also heard you have a parcel."

Craig did a neat about-face, exposing the bundle strapped to his back.

"Is that what I think it is?" Koree queried, with wide eyes.

"Yeah," Craig answered. "This place is getting weirder and weirder."

*****

The electrician knocked on the physician's clinic door.

"I see you have a papoose," Doctor Johnson said. "Come on in. Let's take a gander."

Janis unwrapped the parcel and said, "Exactly as advertised."

"Yeah, it's a boy."

"You fed him?"

"Goat milk from a nipple bottle," Craig replied. "Once at the Halfway Mark. And once on Koree's aircraft. The youngling never made a sound, the whole way."

"What did Koree say?"

"She was too flabbergasted to say much of anything."

"I can imagine," said Janis. "I'm guessing this is the first male child with light skin to ever be born into the fisher-folk clan."

"Yeah, that's my take on it. And Loda said it would keep happening."

"Loda is becoming a prophet, is he?"

"Yeah, it seems that way."

"How did the clan react?"

"They're dumbfounded, to hear Loda tell it."

"Did Loda tell them this would keep occurring?"

"Nope, he thought this youngling was enough of a shocker, as it was."

"Loda is probably right on that score," said Janis. "And it's a good thing he gave us a heads-up. I have everything prepared. What did Aleesa say?"

"She didn't want anything to do with the kid. Rance did his best to sway her, but she was adamant."

"Well, I can't really blame her," said Janis. "Those ladies aren't geared to handle a male child."

"But we are."

"Yes, I have Seth and Josh and Jon on full standby status."

"It takes a village, though," said Craig. "Do you think the youngling will be accepted in Earth Town?"

"I don't see why not. We're all immigrants ourselves."

"Yeah, that's true."

"By the way, what name was given to the child?"

"You're not going to believe this, Doctor. And I swear I'm not making this up. It's no gag."

"What?"

"Adam."

"The irony just gets thicker and thicker, doesn't it?"

"Yeah," the electrician replied. "It certainly does."

43—IT TAKES A VILLAGE

Twice a year, on average, a male child with light skin was ferried from the fisher-folk enclave to Earth Town. Vik and Sluggo and Seth and Josh and Jon, together with every other tenant of Earth Town, undertook the education and nurture of these newcomers.

From the outset, Mayor Martinez decreed that there would be no second-class citizens in Earth Town. And all of the electorate heartily affirmed this edict.

The fisher-folk boys were treated with respect and dignity. Moreover, the lads felt that they were special—that they, like the abandoned girls in the rainforest, had been afforded an opportunity for a better life. Still and all, every boy was expected to do his chores and work hard in school and pull his weight in the neighborhood.

As the population of Earth Town grew, so did the physical plant. Cement was made into concrete on a routine basis. And the fisher-folk boys helped with this construction, as they did with most other activities in the colony.

"I don't savvy," Rance said to Craig. "There's nothing wrong with these kids. Why were they tossed out? Why were they thrown away? When will those fisher-folk dummies wise up? Their way of doing things is goofy. Their reckoning is deranged."

"It's an old story," Craig replied. "Prejudice has ruled Earth for thousands of years. Earthlings looked down on fellow Earthlings, because they were different in some way."

"I know. But it's danged silly."

"It wasn't just skin color, either. It was the way they talked or the way they worshipped or the way they looked. Or they were just plain *in the way*.

"I submit for your consideration: Spain and Portugal. They were once the wealthiest and most powerful nations in Europe. They had everything going for them, including first shot at the prodigious riches of the New World. But then, the Christians of Spain and Portugal threw out their Moorish and Jewish citizenry: Their best and brightest people. And, within a century, Spain and Portugal had become second-tier powers. A century after that, they were among the poorest countries in Europe. And they never recovered."

"I didn't know that, *amigo*."

"It's true, my friend. And male Earthlings constantly kept female Earthlings from achieving their promise. And, in the process, they set back progress for centuries. It was like fighting a battle with one arm, instead of two. It was insipid and pointless. But Earthlings are still doing it, I'll wager."

"Whoa, Nelly. I didn't want you to get up on a soapbox. I'm with you one hundred percent on this. What I'm asking is: Why are folks in the Whistle Stop better than the fisher folk?"

"In all fairness, our benefactors recruited twenty of the best candidates, counting Andy, from thousands of people on two islands, for Earth Town; whereas they had to pull out a whole tribe of idiots, set in their ways, to plunk down in the rainforest. Lunacy is pretty hard to overcome, especially when you yoke it to ignorance."

"You're preaching to the choir, *amigo*. But you might be on target about this recruitment business. I noticed right off the bat that the folks in the Whistle Stop weren't your average Joes and Josephines. I reckon we were picked because we were competent at our jobs and could get along with other folks."

"Yeah, I think so, too. And, if we're smart, we'll keep going the way we're heading."

"If we're smart. That's a big 'if,' *amigo*."

"Yeah, a big 'if.'"

"Do you reckon the fisher folk will ever change?"

"Beats me. Maybe in another century or two they will. But while we're trying to battle prejudice on this planet, we're also harboring hate. You can't blame Aleesa and her sisters for resenting the fisher folk. And you can't blame these boys for resenting the fisher folk, either."

"It's hard to beat hate and resentment."

"Yeah," said Craig. "But, somehow, we have to do it."

44—THE MEMORIAL

Dora and Craig were the singular representatives of Brook Haven in the Forest and Earth Town to show up for the fisher-folk funeral service for Paul.

The couple stood at the periphery of the mourners and respectfully listened to the eulogies.

One of the elders told of the day when the God in the Sky floated by and ordained Paul as the noblest of chieftains.

"Did that really happen?" Dora whispered to Craig, in English.

"Yeah, it went something like that."

"Am I the last to learn everything?"

"Well," said Craig, "I don't know everyone."

"Funny man."

Paul's wives and children and grandchildren stood in front of the crowd, their heads lowered.

"You would have thought that the First Wife would be here," Dora and Craig overheard one fisher-folk female comment, at the ensuing feast.

"Ignore her," Craig said, in English.

"I intend to do so," answered Dora. "Did you hear the story the elder told about when Paul single-handedly killed a giant beast and saved the fisher folk by bringing purple flowers from beyond the mountains?"

"How could I miss it?"

"That's not the way I remember it."

"Me, either. But that's the way it goes. A kernel of fact becomes legend. And the legend grows and changes and finally becomes the accepted version. As Rance puts it: 'They can whittle down a lie, till it's sharp as the truth.'"

"But a few of these people were here on the day that we entered this stronghold with the purple flowers. And I told them that you had killed the giant beast by sending forth bolts of lightning from your hands. Why don't they remember?"

"People are funny, Dora. They believe what they want to believe. But some of them remember. Didn't you see the way Loda rolled his eyes at the retelling?"

"Do you think Loda remembers?"

"I think Loda might be the only one here playing with a full deck."

"Have the rest of them gone nuts?"

"Quite possibly, Dora. In my bygone world, there was also a man named Paul, who was credited with doing something he hadn't done."

"Why didn't the Earthling Paul own up to the lie?"

"He was long dead by then. A storyteller made the Earthling Paul the hero of his story, because, in the future, Earthlings needed a good story and a hero."

"What did the storyteller say the Earthling Paul had done?"

"The storyteller said the Earthling Paul had made a horseback-ride to warn the good people that the bad people were on their way to take away their weapons."

"And the Earthling Paul didn't make the horseback-ride?"

"He gave it a good effort. But the bad people stopped him, before he made much headway."

"How is this a good story?"

"It's a good story because someone else completed the horseback-ride and alerted the good people."

"Why didn't that person get credit for completing the horseback-ride?"

"I don't know. But he was dead, too. So, he couldn't raise a ruckus, could he?"

"Are you making this up?"

"I'm not making this up, Dora. It happened. The first man's name was Paul Revere. And the man who completed the horseback-ride was named Samuel Prescott. And the storyteller was named Henry Wadsworth Longfellow."

"You're inventing this as you go, aren't you?"

"I'll show you in the library, the next time we're in Earth Town."

"Don't think I'll forget."

"I won't."

"Is the truth printed in library books?"

"In most of the books, there's truth."

"Well, if the truth is there, for anyone to read, why does anyone believe lies?"

"Beats me."

"Are the only sane people living in Brook Haven in the Forest and in Earth Town?"

"I think you might be onto something there, Dora."

"How do you know the truth about the Earthling Paul?"

"I do a lot of reading. And I stumbled upon the truth."

"Then, some of the books contain the truth. And other books contain lies?"

"That's right."

"Why are there lies in library books?"

"Anyone can write a book, Dora. And anyone can tell lies. And if you tell a big enough lie, or if you tell a lie often enough, the lie gets believed."

"Even by the person telling the lie?"

"Even by the person telling the lie," Craig attested.

"I don't understand."

"It's human nature."

"You and Rance keep saying that something is *human nature*, whenever someone does something nutty."

"I suspect we do."

"Let's get out of here. My brain is hurting."

"Mendacity does that to brains."

"What's mendacity?"

"Lying."

"Why do people lie?"

"Beats me."

"You and Rance keep saying *beats me*, whenever you can't come up with a good answer."

"I suspect we do."

"I noticed that no one said anything about the time you decked Paul in a fight. Rance said the chieftain went out like a light."

"Well—"

"What are you two talking about?" a tenor phonation, in the woodlander language, inquired from behind.

Dora and Craig pivoted to find Loda in their midst.

"We were speaking of high-minded things," Craig fibbed, in the woodlander tongue.

"This is the day for it," Loda replied.

"Who becomes the chieftain now?" Craig asked the shaman.

"I chose Tohbee."

"Who is Tohbee?" Dora asked.

Loda inclined his head toward the tallest man in the stronghold. "Tohbee is the son of Borg, the oldest elder. Tohbee is a man of much ability. And he will be a good chieftain."

"I am puzzled that Paul died when he did," Craig said. "He was not an old man."

"We are in accord," Loda replied. "Paul had scarcely seen seventy cycles of the stars. He aged faster than he should have done."

"Why is that?" Craig asked.

"It began on the day that he took his daughter, Sara, to Aleesa's Village. A little bit of Paul died then."

Dora knitted her brow, but held her silence.

"I know what you two are thinking," Loda said. "Paul should have let Sara stay here. He should have demanded it. But that is not how things are done in this tribe. We are ruled by conformity and idiocy. Even a great chieftain is powerless against such foes. A chieftain must remain popular. And to be popular, he is sometimes unable to do the right thing, no matter how much it pains him. Popularity is more important here than justice is."

"There is much of your teacher in you, Loda," said Craig. "And that is a good thing."

"We are in accord," Loda answered. "My predecessor was a good shaman. But he was an even better human being.

And I learned a great deal from him about being both. But, as Rance says, in your *lingo*: 'A fat passel of good that does.'"

45—DOUBLE WEDDING

Linda and Nancy noticed that Vik and Sluggo had been spending more and more time at Brook Haven in the Forest. Consequently, they weren't completely caught off guard when word reached them (via Sheela) that the boys had serious girlfriends.

"I saw this coming," said Nancy. "It was bound to happen. After all, the boys are in their twenties."

"That's no excuse," Linda protested. "Victor just turned twenty-eight. In Earth years, he would barely be twenty-six. That's way too young."

"How old are boys on Earth," Sheela politely inquired, "when they get married?"

"Married?" Linda yawped. "Are they that serious?"

"I believe they are," Sheela answered.

Linda stifled a profanity.

"How old are boys on Earth," Sheela asked again, "when they get married?"

"It depends," Nancy replied.

"On what?"

"Oh, things," Nancy vaguely answered.

"What things?"

"Oh, um, things," said Nancy.

"Doesn't your chieftain forbid hanky-panky before marriage?" Linda asked Sheela.

"What's hanky-panky?"

"You know," said Linda, "like holding hands."

"Holding hands?"

"Listen," said Linda, "this is getting us no place. Are the boys talking about getting married?"

"The subject has been broached," Sheela circumspectly replied.

"Why haven't they come to us?" asked Nancy.

"I think that's what they're doing now," said Sheela, "with me acting as their intermediary."

"I see," said Linda.

"Are you against their getting married?" Sheela asked.

"Definitely," Linda answered, before Nancy could get a word in.

"My chieftain is against it," Sheela confided.

"What?" Linda blurted out. "Why?"

"Well, they are, after all, boys. And they are, after all, from the grassland."

"And what's wrong with grassland boys?" Nancy wanted to know.

"Nothing, as far as I'm concerned. But you know my chieftain. She doesn't trust grasslanders."

"But your chieftain married a grasslander," Linda recounted. "She practically shanghaied the guy."

"But my chieftain sees Rance as an exceptional man."

"And our boys aren't exceptional men?" Linda shot back.

"I know they are. And you know they are. But my chieftain—"

"I think we'd better have a talk with your chieftain," Linda enjoined.

"If you believe that's best. When do you want to see her?"

"Is Koree in town?" Nancy asked.

"As a matter of fact, Koree flew me here this morning. And she hasn't gone back, yet."

Linda and Nancy locked eyes.

"I think we should book a flight," Linda postulated.

"Damned straight," Nancy enunciated.

*****

Two weeks later, a double wedding was held in Brook Haven in the Forest. Koree had been flying shuttles all morning. Both dune buggies were parked at the bus stop. Most of the Earth Town constituency, who could be spared from the day's labors, were on hand. Richie the Plumber and Tim the Meat

Cutter, for instance, stayed behind to do the milking for Linda and Chris.

As Aleesa pronounced the words of the wedding ritual, Rance pulled Sheela aside.

"I don't savvy," the hunter said to the healer. "Nancy and Linda don't seem at all miffed by these proceedings."

"Well," said Sheela, "they are a mite put out with Aleesa's attitude."

"But Aleesa wanted this to happen."

"You know that," said Sheela. "And I know that."

"So that's how you got around them, you little minx. Well, tickle me pink. You rainforest damsels are pretty danged sneaky."

"You forget that my father is a grasslander."

"Affirmative," said Rance. "The best of all worlds."

"And the sneakiest," Sheela added.

46—RAISON D'ÊTRE

Following form, Vik and Sluggo spent a few days each month with their spouses in Brook Haven in the Forest. The duo shared a shuttle with older Earth Town husbands, who visited the rainforest to be with their wives and daughters.

Vik and Sluggo might've believed that marrying the women they loved was their idea. But the whole business had been arranged by Sara and Sheela, years before, and had been played out on the playing fields of the flatlands.

Little did the boys realize that they were the equivalent of rooster pheasants during a South Dakota hunting season.

Aleesa and Gloria kept their distance from the machinations.

Aleesa explained to Rance, in English: "Those girls know what they're doing. I would just gum up the works."

"And if anything goes wrong," Rance replied, "you have plausible deniability."

"We are in accord, my husband," the chieftain answered, in the woodlander tongue.

*****

Whenever the boys and girls had met for kickball games and soccer matches, Sara and Sheela arranged for certain girls to be with Vik and Sluggo. After a bit of give-and-take, it was decided which girls would marry which boys. The way the scheme was executed, though, made it all seem spontaneous.

Although Vik and Sluggo never competed in chess tournaments and acted in the capacity of coaches to their youthful charges, Sara and Sheela were careful never to pit Vik and Sluggo and their prospective mates against each other in *impromptu* matches, or even to let them discuss chess—since both women were crack players.

It wouldn't do to bruise the ego of a prospective husband. Such harsh authenticity could wait until after the wedding.

Since Vik and Sluggo possessed pragmatic personalities, no jealousy or rivalry between them was detectable.

Also, the women were level-headed—and they viewed Aleesa and Rance and Dora and Craig as nuptial paradigms.

Within a couple of years, Vik and Sluggo had daughters of their own—both delivered by Sheela, with Nancy and Linda and Doctor Johnson attending.

Although Vik and Sluggo spent a portion of their lives with their new families, much of their attention was devoted to the raising of the Earth Town boys from the fisher-folk enclave. Seth and Josh and Jon, although mature teenagers and capable teachers, welcomed the assistance of their elders.

Each year, two or three male infants were brought to the Earth Town orphanage. Within five years, more than a dozen boys were being boarded there. Already, a nursery and two dormitories had been constructed to house them. And Vik and Sluggo and Seth and Josh and Jon slept in the dorms with their protégés.

Each evening, in both dormitories, before the children went to sleep, one of the mentors declaimed: "Goodnight, you Princes of the Prairie. Sleep tight, you Kings of the New World."

And, although the rainforest orphans didn't quite catch the full meaning of this benediction, which Vik and Sluggo had practically lifted from the library's copy of John Irving's *The Cider House Rules*, the young royals nevertheless felt at peace.

Meanwhile, baby boys and baby girls were being conveyed by Loda and Lin to the Halfway Mark.

Said Craig to Rance, after one such conveyance: "There doesn't seem to be any end to this pattern. Pale-skinned girls in Brook Haven in the Forest; and pale-skinned boys in Earth Town. What the heck are our benefactors are up to?"

"Beats me," replied the hunter. "Do you really reckon those star hoppers have an agenda?"

"I don't think they do anything without a reason."

"But do you find any logic in this?"

"Maybe it's a social experiment," Craig tendered. "Or maybe they're producing a new race of humans."

"You mean hybrid humanity?"

"Yeah, maybe."

"But why?"

"Beats me."

"This is so cockeyed, *amigo*. We have five islands on this spinning rock, with plants and animals from five separate stages of evolution. Six, including us humans. But why? What's it all for?"

"I keep thinking there's a design in all this."

"That's the way with *Homo sapiens*. We tend to look for order in chaos."

"One man's chaos is another man's order."

"Who said that?"

"I just did."

"Oh."

"The thing is, my friend, no matter what's going on, we have to play the hand our benefactors dealt us. It doesn't matter whether it makes sense. We have to keep chugging away and trying our best. For want of a better word, this is our purpose on this planet."

"I reckon you just defined the meaning of life, *amigo*. The difference here is that we're pretty sure that there are supreme beings. But, on Earth, we pretended that there was a Supreme Being. We had faith that there might be one. And we had faith that the Supreme Being cared about us and looked after us. But here, it's more than faith."

"And here, we have faith that the supreme beings are rooting for us to succeed."

"Affirmative, *amigo.* Whatever *success* means to the star hoppers. And we have faith that they won't discard us or wipe us out, if we displease them."

"You mean like Noah and the Ark?"

"Affirmative, *amigo.* Here's to no rivers rising, north or south."

47—ENNUI

Half-a-dozen years after the birth of Adam (the first light-skinned fisher-folk male), statistics changed in the fisher-folk stronghold. Instead of two boys and one girl with light-colored skin being born per annum, only one boy and one girl were thus afflicted (or blessed). And, a decade later, this frequency fell off. A year or two passed, on average, before a light-colored baby was delivered by Loda and Lin to the Halfway Mark.

Nonetheless, there were children to be raised and educated in Brook Haven in the Forest and Earth Town. With a burgeoning population, more trees had to be felled and huts fashioned in the woodland. In Earth Town, more concrete dormitories were erected—and more gardens and orchards and vineyards were planted and nurtured.

The children were expected to earn their keep—and they did so eagerly. No exception or discrimination was to be countenanced in either encampment. Every child learned how to swim and play chess and pound the piano and do the jobs of the adults. Budding plumbers, mechanics, masons, horticulturalists, cooks, bakers, farmers, machinists, blacksmiths, butchers, carpenters, meat cutters, seamstresses, artists, musicians, hunters, anglers, archers, nurses, dentists, and physicians were rife.

Seth and Josh and Jon were duly married to woodland lasses. Yet, most of their days were spent in Earth Town, with Vik and Sluggo, taking care of the younger boys. And, with each passing year, more mentors were graduated.

Although life was going smoothly in Earth Town and Brook Haven in the Forest, all was not well on the other side of the camera—as Craig discovered while visiting with Reginald Wylie (also known as the Tree Spirit).

"Creighton is bored out of his gourd," Reginald imparted to Craig. "He's got *ennui*, as the Frogs call it, leaking from every orifice. He's of little use to me anywise. He sits around and stuffs his cheeks with chocolate biscuits, and swills oolong by the liter, and watches the Beeb for hours."

"The Beeb?" Craig parroted. "Creighton watches television? You mean BBC television from Earth?"

"We accrue the odd shipment of news programming from the Beeb."

"What's going on there? I mean, on Earth?"

"Nothing good," Reginald replied, with a huff. "The place is going bloody bonkers. You're lucky to be out of it, mate."

"But Creighton finds the BBC news entertaining?"

"I should say so."

"But why is he bored with us?"

"You lot don't do anything. You don't wage war. You don't commit crimes. You don't even have an occasional tiff. He finds you a vapid dissatisfaction."

"He wants us to wage war and commit crimes?"

"Mate, I don't have to verse you on the principles of good storytelling, do I? You take likable characters and place them in harm's way."

"Yeah, but isn't that what happened here?"

"It was a brilliant opener. I'll say that for it. There was Rance's Law, for one. We expected the relentless stalker would have to hunt down and dispatch an amiable miscreant, mayhap a best friend, *à la* Owen Wister's *The Virginian*. That would've made for good theater. But, as you know, this didn't come to pass. It didn't even come close to occurring."

"Yeah," said Craig, his intonation dripping with sarcasm. "Too bad about that."

"And we expected you and the jungle giant, Paul by name, to have a running feud. But, nay, mate. You two settled things, once and for all, with a single round of fisticuffs. Where is the pathos in that, I ask you?"

"Not much, I suspect."

"And we looked for an all-out savage skirmish between you lot and the fishermen. But that never came to pass, either. You even got on well with the Amazon lasses."

"Yeah, that's true. We did."

"At the very least, Rance's Rangers could've staged a military coup and taken over the reins of government, as it were. Blimey! The Rangers could be ruling all three hamlets by now."

"Yeah, maybe."

"You even turned racial discrimination to everyone's advantage."

"Yeah, I suspect we did."

"Creighton and I were itching for the Planet of Terror. And you gave us the Planet of the Goody-Two-Shoes."

"Cheer up, chum. Everything could still go to heck in a hand-basket."

"You have to see it from our angle, mate. Creighton and I are documentary filmmakers. We're dedicated to chronicling the unusual, the unsavory, the freakish, the inexplicable, the unthinkable. When you lot were making flights to other islands, we found it to be brilliant theater. Creighton was desirous of a disaster or two along the way. But nothing of the sort came to pass. You lot play it so safe, that nothing untoward is in the mix."

"Did Creighton want a dinosaur to chomp on one of us?"

"It would've made for brilliant viewing."

"For you? Or your bosses?"

"I can't answer for the Boys Upstairs. But Creighton and I would've gotten a giggle out of it."

"It's my opinion that you and Creighton are the sickest puppies I've ever met."

"Be that as it may, actualities aren't pretty. Have you ever watched a nature documentary? They're not for the faint of heart, mate. I mean, we'll show you baby ducks starving to death, followed by a gazelle being brought down by a lioness or a crocodile. As the poet said, Nature is 'red in tooth and claw.'"

"Tennyson."

"Come again?"

"Alfred, Lord Tennyson, wrote that."

"I thought it might've been Wordsworth."

"Nope, it was Tennyson."

"That's a dead cert?"

"Yeah."

"I keep forgetting you used to be a schoolmaster."

"I read every day, too."

"Be that as it may, I must tell you that the flights of discovery you made opened our eyes a smidge."

"What do you mean?"

"We didn't know about the other islands."

"Seriously? You didn't know?"

"We were on a need-to-know basis, mate. And we didn't need to know."

"Then, you're as much in the dark about this setup as we are."

"Spot-on, mate. Full marks. We learned, early on, not to pose interrogatives."

"But you'd think this new knowledge of other islands would've perked Creighton up a tad."

"Oh, it did. But it was a temporary upswing. In our lookout, the less we know, the better off we are."

"I don't get it."

"We're in the business of finding things out, that's true enough. But, in the main, we're interested in ferreting out the bizarre, the sensational. We're not interested in what makes things tick. We're not bloody scientists. We're bloody voyeurs. We're peeping Toms. We pry up rocks to see the dank danger beneath. The danker, the better."

"If Creighton is bored, why aren't you?"

"I can't afford to be, mate. I have to keep the show up-and-running. Creighton doesn't seem to realize that we could be replaced in the twinkling of an eye."

"But you suspect otherwise."

"I know otherwise. The Boys Upstairs merely desire footage. They don't care if it's exciting. In a way, they're more voyeuristic than we are. If Creighton and I fall down on the job, it's curtains for us."

"How do you know that?"

"The Boys Upstairs were looking at two other documentarians, before Creighton and I got the nod. And those blokes were good. Almost as good as we are."

"But that was decades ago. They'd be old men, or dead men, by now."

"You don't follow, mate. The Boys Upstairs aren't fettered by chronology. They can go back and fetch those blokes to replace us."

"I still don't get it."

"They can go back, mate. They can go back in time."

"Your bosses are time travelers?"

"In a manner of speaking, they are. As I apprehend it, the Boys Upstairs exist in all time: Past and present and future."

"I think I know what you mean, Reg. I read about creatures like that."

"You did?"

"Well, granted, it was fiction. But truth is sometimes stranger than fiction."

"And don't I know it."

"But how can you, one person, be handling the duties of two men?"

"Ah, the Boys Upstairs keep providing us with new and better equipment. That's what's keeping me going. As long as I get technological upgrades, I'm good as gold."

"And you don't miss Creighton helping you?"

"The fact is that Creighton has a bit of the bombast about him. He's a grand talker. He got us gigs. But, truth be told, I did much of the work. Creighton mostly got underfoot."

"But don't you fear for Creighton's safety?"

"I get what you're saying, mate. You're afraid Creighton might top himself. Well, believe you me: Creighton loves himself much too much to do that. As long as he has his chocolate biscuits and oolong and the Beeb, he'll be right as rain."

"Really? That's all Creighton wants out of life?"

"Well, mate, biscuits and tea and the telly are all a man really needs, as long as the biscuits and tea are top-drawer. And the Boys Upstairs provide us with the best. And, of course, Creighton watches vintage cinema on the telly. He loves Alec Guinness. Creighton will watch anything with Old Alec in it. Everything from *David Copperfield* to *Bridge on the River Kwai* to *Smiley's People*. A big fan, Creighton is."

"It's all arithmetic, isn't it?"

"What are you on about, mate?"

"Contentment doesn't lie in the multiplication of wealth, but in the subtraction of desires."

"Who said that?"

"I was paraphrasing Thomas Fuller. He was a Cambridge man. Cambridge is near Bedford, you know."

"Always the schoolmaster, aren't you?"

"I suspect you're right, my friend."

"Still, though," said Reginald, "food for thought."

48—THE PASSING

Sara and Craig were on the savanna at sunrise, jogging toward the bus stop, when they noticed Rance emerging from the rainforest. The runners accelerated their pace and hailed the hunter.

Rance halted and vacuously looked about.

The pair drew abreast of Rance, and Craig said: "Is something the matter, my friend?"

"She's gone," the hunter replied, in a cracked voice.

"Who's gone?"

"I woke up because Ginger was whining. Aleesa wasn't breathing. She didn't have a pulse. I tried CPR. Nothing."

Sara gasped.

"I'm sorry," Craig replied. "I'm so sorry."

The electrician had a feeling of *déjà vu*. This had all happened once before, at this very spot. But, in the past, it had been Andy talking to him about Zeena.

*****

By the time Rance and Craig and Sara arrived at Brook Haven in the Forest, the word had gone out. A swarm of women were gathered around the chieftain's hut. And a few more females, including Dora, were inside, preparing the body for burial.

Separate from the bevy were Ginger, the golden-brown, short-haired, mid-size mongrel dog, and her nearly grown pup. When Ginger smelled Rance, she padded over to him. The pup followed.

Ginger and the pup stayed with Rance and Craig for the remainder of the day, and accompanied them to the Sacred Knoll in the evening. The service was brief and bittersweet.

Craig and Dora and Rance and Ginger and the pup lingered silently by the graveside, after everyone else had departed.

Sara was present, too, but kept a discreet distance from the others.

The six of them returned to the commune, without making a sound, and went their respective ways—Ginger and the pup with Rance—and Craig with Dora.

"What will Rance do now?" Dora asked her spouse, in English.

"We talked about it," Craig answered. "He's going to Earth Town, at least for a while. He and I are catching a ride with Koree tomorrow."

"Do you want me to come with you?"

"No, Dora. You will be needed here."

"Why do you say that, my husband?"

"You knew Aleesa the longest. Except for Rance, you were her best friend. People will want to talk with you."

"I reckon you're right. I hadn't thought about that."

"Ginger and her pup will need you, too."

"I hadn't thought of them, either. Where will they live now?"

"I can't say for certain, Dora. But I wouldn't be at all shocked if they moved in with Sara."

And this is exactly what happened.

*****

Forasmuch as Dora was the oldest of the woodland sorority and had spent more time with Aleesa than anyone else, all of the sisters now deferred to Dora.

But it was a foregone conclusion that Sara would be the new chieftain—whether she liked it or not.

"I cannot see myself as chieftain," Sara said to Dora, in the woodlander tongue.

"I know what you mean," Dora replied. "Aleesa felt the same way, when Zeena died."

"It will not be the same," said Sara.

"I know. But that is not necessarily a bad thing."

"You will stay with me, will you not, Dora? I shall need your counsel, in the coming days."

"I am going nowhere, Sara. You can depend on me. I shall be here for you and my other sisters."

"It is a strange thing, Dora. I always felt so sure of myself. But, at present, I feel shaken, shaken to the roots."

"I feel that way, too, my sister. We have suffered a great loss."

*****

After a few weeks of mourning had subsided, Sara and Ginger and the pup took up residence in the chieftain's lodgings.

Ginger and the pup accompanied Sara everywhere. But when Sara was away from the settlement, the dogs gravitated toward Dora.

Craig sometimes entertained the notion that these canines, especially Ginger, somehow recognized that Dora was going to be around for the long haul.

"Dogs have a sixth sense," Craig told his wife, in English. "Ginger seems to know that you won't let her down."

"Is that something dogs can do?" asked Dora.

"I believe so," Craig answered.

And another chapter in the saga of Brook Haven in the Forest drew to a close.

49—DESOLATE DORA

My sisters are growing older and dying," Dora said to Craig, in the woodlander tongue. "But I am doing neither."

"This is true," her spouse answered.

"And it is not a good thing," Dora closed her critique. "Whenever my friends die, I am greatly saddened."

"It is the way of the world, Dora. But you are constantly meeting new sisters and making new friends."

"Only to have them eventually die. What is the purpose of that?"

Craig bowed his head. "I know it hurts when friends pass away. And there seems to be no purpose to it."

"But why am I not growing older?"

Craig knew the answer. In a moment of weakness, he had committed, what he now knew to be, a selfish act. He had given his wife an elixir which severely slowed the aging process. And he regretted having done this.

He considered it, however, providential that Dora did not connect drinking the elixir with her inability to age at a normal rate.

"Is it the leaves I eat?" she asked Craig.

"I do not believe that the leaves can prolong life," her spouse replied.

"Then, what is doing it?"

"There is much that we do not know," Craig inveigled. "There are inquiries that we might never be able to answer. We must simply face the facts and accept what is happening."

"How long will I live?"

"Beats me," Craig replied, in English. "But some people would be quite pleased to remain young."

"Who, my husband?" Dora asked, in the woodlander tongue. "Who would want to remain young?"

"While it is true that none of your sisters wants to remain young, I was speaking of people in my bygone world. Many of them sought youth and *immortality*."

"What is immortality?"

"It means that," Craig lapsed into English again, "they wanted to live forever."

"Forever?"

"It's like the people who wrote the words you read in the books we have. Those authors are no longer alive. But they live on, through their writings. It's like the musicians who wrote and performed the music we listen to. They live on, when we hear their music."

"I understand this, my husband, and it seems natural. But living forever, in a physical body, does not seem natural."

"We are in accord, Dora. Immortality isn't natural, although there is at least one creature I know of that lives forever: The jellyfish."

"What is a jellyfish?"

"Jellyfish live in water. But there are no jellyfish in our rivers. Jellyfish, if they live in this world, live in the big water beyond the rivers."

"Is that the one creature that lives forever?"

"Some tortoises live longer than human beings can."

"What are tortoises?"

"Tortoises are slow-moving creatures. They have a rock-hard protection about them. This protection is their home. And they carry their home with them wherever they go."

"Are there any tortoises here?"

"There might be tortoises in other parts of this world, but not in our valley."

"Is anything else immortal?"

Craig gestured upward. "The stars and sun and moons live forever. Well, maybe not forever. But pretty close to forever."

"I understand this, my husband. It is natural. But people should not live forever. It is heartbreaking. And it is not natural."

"Who is to say what is natural?" Craig countered. "Most things are ordinary. Most things are understandable. But there are some things that are not ordinary or understandable."

"I keep the memory of Zeena in my heart. And she remains alive to me."

"Truly, this is so."

"That is ordinary. That is natural. That is understandable."

"Most people in my bygone world wanted to live forever. But that made no sense, because, for much of their lives, they were bored."

"What is bored?"

"Bored means being tired of life, Dora. It means not being interested in living."

"I see. It makes no sense to live forever, if you are bored with living."

"Have you ever been bored?"

"I was always interested in what I was doing."

"That is the wonder of this world," Craig said. "There is always something of interest. And it doesn't take long to find it."

50—CENTENNIAL

Craig traipsed to Andy's Quonset hut, which had once been the electrician's domicile, and knocked on the door.

The god greeted him and swept him inside.

"What brings you to this burg?" Andy inquired.

"I just dropped off another fisher-folk youngling," Craig replied.

"How many does that make for us now?"

"I'm not certain, my friend. I've lost count."

"The more the merrier, brother. That's what I say."

"I suspect everyone agrees with you."

"There's plenty of room for growth here."

"Yeah, it's a spacious prairie."

"True that."

"There's one thing we never had to keep track of."

"What's that?"

"We never had to know who the parents of these children were."

"You mean that's changed?"

"Yeah, think about it. The light-skinned boys from the fisher folk and the light-skinned girls from the fisher folk will someday be meeting and marrying."

"Oh," said Andy. "I see where you're going with this. We can't have siblings accidentally marrying siblings. Or cousins, either."

"Yeah, who knew that was going to be a problem?"

"I, for one, never considered the possibility."

"Now, I have to keep records of information we didn't want to know before."

"Yes, before, we were better off not knowing."

"And speaking of knowledge," said Craig, "while I was in Doctor Johnson's office, she told me something I didn't know."

"What's that?"

"She tells me that we've been on this planet for one hundred years now."

"Is that one hundred Earth years?"

"Nope, it's one hundred of this planet's years."

"Still, I wouldn't have guessed."

"Me, either. But the good doctor, as you know, keeps good records. So, I have confidence in her count."

"If I have the arithmetic right, one hundred years here, would be about ninety years back home."

"Back home," Craig iterated. "That sounds strange, doesn't it? I've been a resident of this world far longer than I resided on Earth. This planet is home for me now."

"We should have a celebration."

"You're probably right, my friend. But what could we do? It's not as though Earth Town has any real shindigs, to speak of. The closest we come is movie night and music concerts and dramatic productions and athletic events. And, after the harvest is done, we try to celebrate. But we're really too exhausted to properly pull it off."

"But we give it a shot, anyway."

"Yeah, we give it a shot."

"We've never had a holiday here, as far as I know. We don't even do weekends. We don't even know when our birthdays are."

"Yeah, in a way, that's sad."

"You know what this means, don't you?"

"What?"

"We're more than a hundred years old, you and I, even factoring in Earth years."

"Yeah."

"And all of us who married rainforest women have had our wives die, except for you."

"Yeah."

"And none of us widowers ever got remarried."

"Yeah."

"And, nowadays, when the settlers of Earth Town go to the women's burg, it's to visit their children and grandchildren and great-grandchildren and great-great grandchildren."

"Yeah, when we first arrived on this planet, I told the Earth Town men that there was no such thing as divorce for the woodland women. And, it turns out, there's no such thing as remarriage, either."

"Why would that be?"

"I don't think anyone thought about it. I think it was taken for granted. You get married once on this planet. And it's for keeps."

"Not a bad way to live, brother."

"Yeah, I think you're right."

"I asked Mike about it."

"You did? What did he say?"

"He told me he lost interest in erotic love, after his wife died. He said the other men felt the same way, after their wives died."

"They lost interest, huh?"

"That's what Mike said."

"It might be something our benefactors chemically engineered. It might've been in the longevity juice they gave us, on our migration here."

"That's a possibility. But, you know, we might all, by nature, be one-woman men."

"Yeah, there's that."

"You know what?"

"What?"

"I miss Koree."

"She did a great job flying the *Albatross II* all those years, didn't she?"

"Yes, she was one of a kind."

"Yeah, she was one of the best."

"Does Sara still run with you?"

"Not for a while now. She remains nimble, though. And she's still up to the job of being chieftain. But she's looking her age."

"She never got married, did she?"

"Nope."

"And Loda is still the shaman?"

"Yeah, but I can tell that he's getting on in years. He lets Lin do all of the heavy lifting."

"Good for him. Smart fellow."

"And Ginger has raised three puppies, and one kitty."

"Yes, that dog has known heartache."

"We all have, my friend. I believe Dora is right about our living this long. It's not good for the heart, to know so much loss."

"It is hard, isn't it?"

"Yeah."

"If anything does kill us, brother, I'm supposing it will be heartache."

"Yeah."

"They say it's better to have loved and lost, than to have never loved at all."

"But is that true? I don't think so."

"Who did say that? I mean, originally."

"Alfred, Lord Tennyson."

"I thought it might've been Wordsworth."

"Nope, it was Tennyson."

"Is there anything you don't know?"

"I read every day."

"Yes, the library's books are keeping me sane."

"And you're still writing your book, aren't you? *Andy's Annals*, I once called it."

"Yes, *Andy's Annals*. Catchy title. But, of course, no one refers to it as that."

"What do they call it?"

"You're not going to believe this."

"What?"

"It's referred to as *The Bible*."

"I'll be darned. Who calls it that?"

"The younger generations."

"Don't they know there's already a Bible?"

"I don't suppose they do, brother. We have a few copies of the actual Bible in the library. But no one, except us old-timers, bothers to look at them."

"Where, then, did they get the name, *The Bible*?"

"I'm guessing they've heard the title as an idiom. You know, this manual or that text is 'the Bible' on this or that."

"Yeah, I suspect you're right."

"But the word, *biblia*, in Greek and Latin, means *books*, or *a collection of books*. So, in a sense, you could call this scribbling of mine a Bible.

"Is your Bible finished?"

"No, I have a feeling I'll be working on it, right up until I cast off this mortal coil."

"That wouldn't be such a bad thing, you know. Your Bible has a lot of enlightenment in it already. If anything, it chronicles our story here."

"Yes, there's useful data in there. I just don't want it to become required reading for those-to-come."

"It probably should be required reading. Knowledge is important. But wisdom is even more important. The human inhabitants of this island, in the coming centuries, could use your Bible as a guide for both."

"Listen to us, brother, talking about the future. We have no idea how long we're going to live. Do I have another century in me? I don't suppose so. But who knows?"

"Yeah."

"Remember when they used to call you The Old Man?"

"Yeah."

"Now, we're all old men, and women."

"Yeah, it's a brave new world, all right. And who knows what will happen next?"

"True that, brother."

51—LIFE REQUIREMENTS

The electrician and the deity had adjourned to *Hank's and Frank's*, where they were sipping coffee and nibbling doughnuts, when the god piped up: "You've probably heard of the Drake Equation, which says that, based on the sheer preponderance of numbers of planets, life must exist throughout the galaxy."

"Yeah," Craig replied. "I've heard of it."

"Well," said Andy, "numbers alone are meaningless. The search for sustained life is not like looking for a four-leaf clover in a cow pasture, or looking for a needle in a haystack. It's more like combing all of the gravel pits in all of the world, and coming up with a raw diamond. That isn't going to happen."

"Yeah, probably not."

"Let's say that you and I were playing cards. And we had two dozen sealed decks. And you opened the deck boxes, one by one, and shuffled the cards and cut the deck. And I dealt you four aces. And then I dealt myself a straight flush to the king. And I accomplished this feat two dozen consecutive times, with two dozen different decks. What would you say are the odds of that happening?"

"I'd say it was impossible. If it happened once, that would be extraordinary. But if it happened two or three times in a row, I'd say a magician was manipulating the cards."

"And you'd be right, brother. And yet, this is what happened to Earth."

"What do you mean?"

"Take solar systems."

"What about them?"

"Earth's solar system is unique. Most solar systems have two or three or four, or more, stars in them. So, their planets have cockamamie orbits. One month, a typical planet is a snowball. The next month, it's a fiery Hell."

"Yeah, I can see that."

"And those rare single-star solar systems don't ordinarily have the kind of sun we had on Earth. And Earth's sun, which is called a *yellow dwarf*, has gone through phases. The planet Earth got under way as a pile of cold rocks which coalesced into a molten orb. Then, it was a snowball, at least twice. And, someday, Earth's yellow dwarf sun will expand and immolate the inner planets. So, timing is crucial."

"Yeah, I can see that."

"Earth's solar system came by its ninety-four natural elements from the explosion of a supernova. Without that supernova explosion, life on Earth would've been impossible."

"Why is that?"

"All of the elements essential to life proceed from supernova explosions. A yellow dwarf sun, alone, can produce hydrogen and helium in large quantities, plus a few other elements in small quantities. But that's it."

"I did not know that."

"Another vital requirement is that your planet has to be a small rock planet. Not a gas giant."

"Yeah, that makes sense."

"And even if your small rock planet is the right distance from the right kind of sun, and the sun doesn't vary in size or brightness, you still need a long list of vital requirements."

"Such as?"

"Your planet has to have a stable and elliptical revolution, which can't be too long or too short."

"Yeah, I can see that."

"Your planet has to have a stable rotation, at the right speed."

"Yeah, I can see that, too."

"Your planet has to have a water ocean with currents, to move hot air and cold air around the globe. Otherwise, half of your planet will become ice, while the other half will become a broiling desert."

"Yeah, that makes sense."

"Your planet has to have an axial tilt, for the planet to have seasons. And the tilt has to be around twenty-three or twenty-four degrees. Because, if your planet doesn't have seasons, it turns into either a snowball or a fireball."

"Yeah, that makes sense."

"Your planet has to have at least one moon, of adequate size, to stabilize the planet and its degree of axial tilt."

"Yeah, I can see that."

"Your moon has to be the right size and the right distance away, otherwise you have daily tsunamis or no tides at all. And tide pools are probably where life got started on Earth."

"Yeah, that's what I've read."

"Your planet's moon has to have enough gravity to be like a catcher's mitt, snatching incoming meteors and asteroids and comet debris. Earth's airless moon gets hit by tons of celestial projectiles every single day. Some are the size of fifty-caliber slugs, traveling faster than a speeding bullet. Others are huge enough to make craters, visible from Earth. It's better to have this stuff hit the moon than your planet."

"Yeah, I totally agree."

"Your planet has to have tectonic plates above a thick and fluid mantle, to shove around land masses, and create mountains and volcanoes, and trap carbon dioxide in rocks. Mountains alter and stabilize climates. Magma brings up vital minerals from underground and creates new land. Volcanic soil, you know, is the most fertile on Earth. And geothermal energy warms water and turns turbines to generate electricity. Without plate tectonics, you end up with Venus."

"Yeah, that's what I've read."

"Your planet has to have an atmosphere. And that atmosphere has to have nitrogen and oxygen and carbon and hydrogen and sulfur and phosphorus, and in the right proportions. And the atmosphere has to be high enough and thick enough to protect living things from cosmic radiation and ultraviolet rays and meteors and asteroids and comets and other space invaders."

"Yeah, that makes sense."

"Your planet has to have an ozone layer, to absorb deadly solar radiation."

"Yeah, that makes sense."

"Your planet has to have a magnetosphere, made possible by the presence of iron and nickel, rotating within a hot inner core that generates strong electromagnetic fields. This shields the planet from solar and cosmic particle radiation and solar winds. Without a magnetosphere, you end up with Mars."

"Yeah, I read that Mars lost most of its atmosphere to solar winds."

"Yes, and your planet has to have gravity. Not too much gravity and not too little. Too much gravity crushes you. Too little gravity can't hold onto an atmosphere."

"Yeah, that makes sense."

"And gravity depends on a planet's size and density. Your planet has to have size and density in the right proportions, too."

"Yeah, I can see that."

"Your solar system has to have a giant gas planet, like Jupiter. The tremendous gravity of Jupiter protects Earth from collisions with comets and asteroids. Jupiter, like Earth's moon, serves as a catcher's mitt. Or else it slings comets and asteroids away from your planet."

"Yeah, Earth lucked out there."

"And do you recollect that I told you that Vik and Sluggo had found a Jupiter-like planet here with their telescope?"

"Yeah, I do. That's interesting, isn't it?"

"Yes, it surely is. And your solar system must be stable. And the orbits of other planets have to be predictable. You don't want planets colliding with each other, or being ejected from the system. And you don't want objects from outside your system coming in and wrecking planetary order."

"Nope, that would never do."

"And much depends upon your solar system's location in the galaxy. You have to be far enough away from supernovas and neutron stars and quasars and blazars and star collisions and galaxy collisions and gamma ray bursts and deadly radiation."

"Yeah."

"And you have to be far enough away from the massive black hole, which exists in the center of most galaxies. Earth's sun is on the outer edge of one of the bigger galaxies in the universe. So, it's in a privileged position, way out in the suburbs."

"Yeah, it's like they say in the real estate game: Location, location, location."

"You said it, brother. Many galaxies have much more active centers than the Milky Way has. Some nuclei are extremely hot and bright and deadly. The Milky Way center is, by comparison, reserved."

"Yeah, that's good for us."

"The Milky Way is a safe distance from lethal gamma ray bursts. One of those flares, fired directly at Earth, could take out the whole planet."

"Yeah, Earth got lucky there, too."

"And small black holes, some the size of bowling balls, albeit lethal, exist everywhere in galaxies. But not near Earth. Oh, there might be one out by Pluto. But it really doesn't affect the third rock from the sun."

"I did not know that."

"And then your planet must somehow dredge up nucleic acids, to make DNA. And you need amino acids, to build proteins."

"Yeah, that makes sense."

"If your planet lacks even one of these requirements to sustain life, it's game over."

"Yeah, I'll go along with that."

"And even after meeting all of these requirements, life on Earth was nearly snuffed out on five occasions, which we know about. Ninety-nine percent of all species, which ever lived on Earth, are extinct. They're completely gone, as though they never existed."

"Then, you're saying that sustained life on Earth is more than an aberration. It's darned near impossible to achieve in a galaxy. Any galaxy."

"Exactly. There might not be a single other place in the universe where life could emerge and survive and sustain."

"Then, you think our benefactors are magicians, manipulating life-requirement cards?"

"That's my hypothesis, brother. I doubt that any of the life here was produced locally. It was all brought from Earth."

"Even the panthers? The elbastak?"

"Why not? We don't know where they're from, or even in what time frame on Earth they might have existed. They might even come from Earth's future."

"You're saying our benefactors are time travelers?"

"I suppose they're capable of anything, brother."

"Yeah, I agree."

"You do?"

"Yeah, I've heard this time-traveler charge. And I think I can make it stick."

"Fascinating."

"Do you think this planet was manufactured?"

"As far as I can tell, this entire solar system might be manufactured. And it follows all of the rules for life on Earth. One of my hypotheses is that the islands on this planet were created the same way the Hawaiian Islands were. Like on Earth, there's a hot spot beneath the mantle of this planet. The crust moves over the hot spot. And, every so often, the hot spot breaks through a weak area in the crust and forms another island."

"Oh. So, that's the way it works."

"Yes, and on Earth, the Hawaiian archipelago consists of one hundred thirty-seven islands, stretched across fifteen hundred miles. I looked it up in the library. And the archipelago moved north of the Tropic of Cancer and worked its way diagonally toward the equator. Of course, the plate was moving northwest, in the opposite direction."

"If this were Earth, which Hawaiian island would we be on?"

"We'd be on Oahu. The Permian would be on the Big Island. The Triassic would be on Maui. The Jurassic would be here on Oahu. The Cretaceous would be on Kauai. And the Pleistocene would be on Nihoa."

"Nihoa?"

"On Earth, Nihoa is the next northwestern Hawaiian island, of any size, after Kauai. But, as I told you, our five islands here are the size of Earth's Wisconsin, which makes them much bigger than the Big Island of Hawaii."

"How much bigger?"

"I looked it up in the library. Wisconsin is about sixteen times the size of the Big Island of Hawaii."

"I'm impressed."

“Me, too, brother. I figure our island is right on this planet’s equator.”

“How come?”

“The position of the sun in the sky, plus the fact that we don’t have any severe storms. Hurricanes don’t happen on an equator. It has to do with the Coriolis Effect. I looked that up in the library, too.”

“I did not know that.”

“Most people don’t.”

“Would you then call our magician benefactors a life form?”

“They’re surely a life force, brother. But I don’t know if you can say they’re alive. Not in the way we view life. They might be pure-energy beings.”

“Are you saying our benefactors are gods?”

“What difference does it make what we call them? The main thing is that they probably arranged this whole scenario.”

“What do you mean?”

“You know that each of the islands I visited on this planet is full of animals and plants from various eras from Earth’s past. And there’s no mixing.”

“You mean that our benefactors brought this life from Earth’s past: The Permian, the Triassic, the Jurassic, the Cretaceous, and the Pleistocene?”

“Yes.”

“Why? Why would they do that?”

“It’s an experiment, brother. They wanted to know what would have happened in these epochs of Earth’s history, if evolution hadn’t been impeded by some cataclysmic event, or a series of events, or a virus-like parasite-predator. And by virus-like parasite-predator, I refer to humankind.”

“But such an experiment would have to go on for millions of years.”

“True that. But our benefactors see time differently than we do. You told me that much, yourself. They can live in the moment. And they can also live in geological time.”

“But wouldn’t that make them gods?”

“Again, brother, the nomenclature is unimportant. Let’s call them super-architects, for the sake of argument. These super-architects have successfully created Worlds of If. What would happen, they asked themselves, if they set these animals and plants apart and watched them from a distance?”

“Worlds of If,” said Craig. “That’s catchy.”

“Yes, *Worlds of If* was the name of a twentieth-century science-fiction periodical.”

“I did not know that.”

“Yes, it was a pretty good magazine, too.”

“But getting back to the subject at hand, my friend: What about saltwater creatures from different epochs? Wouldn’t they mix?”

"Our benefactors might even be able to keep saltwater animals, from different eras, apart from each other, too."

"But how?"

"Perchance they use underwater barriers. If they could devise an entire solar system, a force field of that magnitude would be child's play."

"Yeah."

"And that's why there are no flying creatures here, except for the tree gliders. Our benefactors didn't want the land animals migrating and mixing, even by air. Although the islands are far apart, a strong flyer might be able to emigrate. And that would ruin the experiment."

"But they could put a barrier in the air to stop a strong flyer, couldn't they?"

"Yes, but then, how did the *Albatross II* penetrate those barriers? Unless the barriers were temporarily removed to admit our passage."

"Yeah, there's that."

"Fascinating, huh?"

"Then you're saying that our benefactors created Worlds of If to see what would happen to different groups of animals and plants? And they only had Earth to work from, because there's no sustained life anywhere else in the Milky Way galaxy?"

"That's my hypothesis, brother. Do you have a better one?"

"Nope, I can't say I do. But it seems like a lot of trouble for our benefactors to go to."

"Perchance our benefactors suppose it's worth their while. Or perchance they were listless, and supposed it might be fun."

"But that seems silly, for creatures of such giant intellects."

"But what's silly about it, brother? Our intellects don't approach theirs."

"Yeah, but—"

"It's like what the *Old Testament* deity told the Biblical character, Job. And I'm paraphrasing here: 'Who are you to question my actions, when you have so little knowledge of even your own?'"

"That's a simplistic interpretation, my friend. I suspect most theologians would lodge protests."

"But what makes a theologian any good? They're not even talking about anything that's real."

"Yeah, that's a fair argument."

"I'm recollecting what Mark Twain wrote in *Notes from the Earth*."

"I haven't read that book."

"Most folks haven't. It was withheld from publication for decades after his death."

"Why?"

"The book was too controversial. You see, in *Notes from the Earth*, God tells His archangels that He has created animals. And Satan, who was an archangel in Heaven back then, asks God why He did this. And God answers that it's an experiment. So, Satan goes to Earth to observe the outcome of this divine experiment. And Satan comes to the conclusion that all of nature is irrational, especially human beings."

"Yeah, I can't find fault with that appraisal."

"We see our species as the culmination of Mother Nature's tinkering. We see ourselves as the ultimate species. Because we outlived the dinosaurs, we suppose we're more suited to inherit the Earth. But we're not really the all-time champs. Ninety-nine percent of the species, which came before *Homo sapiens*, died because of forces beyond their control. Humans aren't Nature's last word. They're the fortunate survivors. That's all. Humans aren't better suited than the dinosaurs were. Humans just got lucky. Life is endlessly inventive. The tinkering goes on. But there's no idea of progress. It's just a crap shoot. The dinosaurs crapped out. And humans didn't."

"Then, humanity is what remains, after the dice have been rolled a few times?"

"That's the way I see it, brother. There's no survival of the fittest. It's just survival of the luckiest."

52—SONS OF GOD

A few weeks later, Andy once again met with Craig in *Hank's and Frank's* for coffee and doughnuts.

"Can you believe we're having a centennial celebration after all?" the god asked the electrician.

"Nope," said Craig. "You could've knocked me over with a tachyon emission, when I heard the news."

"Did you fly here?"

"Nope, the shuttle was too crowded. It seems that Earth Town is currently hosting a kickball game and a soccer match and a track-and-field meet and a chess tournament and two dramatic productions and three music concerts."

"Are you participating in the sporting events?"

"Nope, I'm not much interested in sports. And I had to hoof it here, so I'm beat. I'm not as young as I used to be, you know."

"You couldn't prove it by me, brother. You look great."

"Take my word for it: I'm bushed."

"What have you been up to lately?"

"I've been musing on eternity."

"You mean like the eternity of a Catholic wedding?"

The electrician visually communicated his amusement. "Yeah, in a way. What have you been up to, my friend?"

"I've been logging more hours in the library."

"Why? Do you have another hypothesis?"

"As a matter of fact, I do."

"Let's hear it."

"You know how we Earthlings woke up in this world, and we found out that we'd been freighted light years away from Earth. In fact, you delivered the news. And I was the last to hear it."

"Yeah, that seems eons ago."

"Doesn't it, though? And we found out we can live for a very long time. Not forever, mind you. But much longer than the Earthly three-score-and-ten."

"Yeah, that's the word on the prairie."

"And our male offspring are also living past this Earthly age limit."

"Yeah, it seems that way."

"Well, I've been reading the Bible. The Hebrew Bible, I mean. *The Book of Genesis*, to be succinct. There's a passage in the sixth chapter. It goes like this: 'There were giants in the earth in those days; and also after that, when the sons of God came in unto the daughters of men, and they bore children to them, the same became the mighty men which were of old, men of renown.'"

"Yeah, I'm familiar with the passage."

"That's *The King James Version* of the Bible. But *The New Revised Standard Version* goes like this: 'The *Nephilim* were on the earth in those days, and also afterward, when the sons of God went in to the daughters of humans, who bore children to them. These were the heroes that were of old, warriors of renown.'"

"Yeah, if I remember my Hebrew rightly, *Nephilim* means *fallen ones*."

"That's right, brother. I keep forgetting you're a polyglot."

"Yeah, but a fat passel of good it does me."

"Well, *The New Revised Standard Version* passage inspired me to ask myself: What if we Earthlings, we newly arrived Earthlings, are the *Nephilim*, the fallen ones, the giants in the earth? And our offspring are the heroes of old, the warriors of renown."

"What makes you think that?"

"The first few generations of humans, according to *The Book of Genesis*, lived for hundreds of years, Methuselah being the oldest. He lived to be 969 years of age."

"You're saying, we're the giants? The founders of Earth Town are the giants?"

"Yes, to some extent. And what if we end up living for hundreds of years?"

"I don't know."

"And what if our benefactors did this all, once before? What if this is the second experiment? Or perchance we're in a long series of such experiments?"

"That sounds wacky."

"I know it does, brother. But hear me out. We live far longer than the woodlanders do. And the woodlanders see us as gods. They see us as mighty warriors. And we had sexual intercourse with their women. Of course, the big difference in these two stories is that one of the woodlander women became a goddess."

"You're referring to Dora."

"Yes, I suppose Dora might be part of this grand experiment. And our benefactors are seeing what will happen, if they tinker with a few variables here and there. In other words, we're reliving the past, with a few new wrinkles."

"What do you think will happen?"

"I'm hoping things will turn out better than they did in the Hebrew Bible. God wanted to wipe out humanity, because He saw them as a blighted *brouillon*. So He flooded the Earth."

"*Brouillon*? You're studying French now?"

"It's a good word, isn't it? It means *trial balloon*."

"Yeah."

"Anyway, this time, God might approve of our actions, and see this trial balloon as a success."

"And you see our benefactors as being God?"

"It's one viewpoint, brother. But keep in mind that the writers of the Hebrew Bible were seeing their world and history in certain contexts. How they saw things, well, they weren't necessarily the way things were. But they described it as best they could, with the intellectual tools they had at hand."

"That's quite a hypothesis, my friend."

"Isn't it, though? And there's one more thing. In the Hebrew Bible, the Creator is sometimes referred to as *Elohim.*"

"So?"

"So, *Elohim*, like *Nephilim*, is a plural word. *Elohim* means *great ones* or *powerful ones* or *mighty ones*."

"And you're thinking that *Elohim* is another way of saying *The Glittering Gods*?"

"It's part of my hypothesis, yes."

"Yeah, I can see that. And there's one more thing about our benefactors."

"What's that?"

"They have a different slant on time than we do. It's so different that I don't think we'll ever be able to comprehend it. But what it comes down to is that they never lose interest in the future or the past, even though they might already know how both of them turn out."

"That's mind-boggling, brother."

"The Glittering Gods put me in mind of Kurt Vonnegut's Tralfamadorians."

"You mean like in *Slaughterhouse Five*?"

"Yeah, the Tralfamadorians exist at all times, at the same time. And nothing fazes them. They know what's going to happen. And they let it happen. They don't interfere. They don't try to change anything, even a catastrophe. They know how their civilization will end. Yet, they don't try to fend off the apocalypse. They are a part of the world. But they're also apart from it."

"Yes, it's a concept beyond human understanding."

"Yeah, it really is."

"What's your take on it?"

"Well, as I told you, I've been musing about eternity."

"Yes?"

"I read a novel by Susan Ertz. In it, she said: 'Millions long for immortality who do not know what to do with themselves on a rainy Sunday afternoon.'"

Andy chuckled. "Yes, that describes a multitude of people I knew on Earth."

"The thing is that I've always known what I wanted to do on a rainy Sunday afternoon."

"Me, too, brother."

"For a scholar, there is no boredom, as long as there are things to learn and study."

"True that."

"But, what if our compatriots on this planet aren't as lucky as we are? What if they lose interest down the line? Will they get bored?"

"Good question."

"And being bored, will it be a kind of death for them? Will they literally get bored to death?"

"Do you suppose they'll get bored enough to end their suffering?"

"I wouldn't blame them if they did."

"Me, either."

"The problem is that we humans see time as linear and absolute and constantly running out. Time is how we organize our lives."

"Then, what's the solution?"

"If time is routine, it becomes meaningless and dull. The trick is to get rid of the routine. You can do the same thing over and over and over. But it has to feel different each time. It has to feel like a new experience. You have to notice something you haven't noticed before. Each day, each hour, each moment can be different, if we choose to make it so."

"Is that possible?"

"Yeah, I think so. If you read a book again or see a movie again, it's different. The book hasn't changed. The movie hasn't changed. But you've changed. You're different. Your experience is different. It's like Heraclitus of Ephesus once said: 'You can't wade into the same river twice.' And just as you can't wade into the same river twice, you can't live the same day twice."

"Good old Heraclitus," said Andy. "He was onto something there. The water is different. And so is the wader."

"I keep thinking of Homer's *Odyssey*."

"What about it?"

"In *The Odyssey*, the nymph Calypso tries to convince Odysseus to live with her forever on her private island, with romance and luxury and eternal youth as his rewards. But Odysseus keeps turning down Calypso, even though the nymph has already borne him two sons. The poor gob yearns to go home to his aging wife and his faithful mutt and his crummy little kingdom by the sea."

"And the morale of the story?"

"People aren't meant to live forever, my friend. And they're inextricably tied to the past."

"I'm reminded of something Francis Scott Fitzgerald wrote in *The Great Gatsby*."

"What's that?"

"So we beat on, boats against the current, borne back ceaselessly into the past."

"Yeah," said Craig. "That pretty much says it all."

53—REGINALD'S FAREWELL

Craig was absorbed in his customary morning constitutional on the outskirts of the rainforest, when he heard the tonic accent of Reginald Wylie in the empty air.

"Do you have a mo, mate?" the unseen Tree Spirit inquired.

Craig skidded to a stop and replied: "Yeah, certainly. What's up, Reg?"

The filmmaker materialized ten feet away and four feet off the ground. "I came to bid you cheery-bye, mate."

Reginald descended an invisible stairway to the stubby steppe grass.

"You're saying so-long?" Craig queried.

"My time has come."

"But you look fine, Reg. Not a day over forty, if that."

"Oh, I know. But I'm feeling creaky. And, you see, Creighton passed."

"When did this happen?" the startled electrician asked.

"It's been a month, give or take."

"Why didn't you tell me before now?"

"Well, there were things to do, people to see, preparations to make."

"How old was Creighton?"

"As to that, Creighton and I were on this planet long before you lot came on the scene. I calculate, all in all, that he'd hung on for seven hundred years, give or take. But I lost track."

"How did it happen? How did he die?"

"It was nothing dramatic. Creighton put down a cup of oolong on the side table. And he slumped over in the sofa. I saw him do it. But I resolved that he'd fallen asleep, as he'd done ever so many times previously. It wasn't till a few hours had gone by that I got up the gumption to check his breathing and his pulse."

"I'm very sorry to hear of Creighton's passing. I liked him."

"Mate, you said we were sick puppies."

"Well, yeah, I did say that. But if it weren't for you and Creighton, we Earthlings would've been in a real fix."

"I appreciate the approbation, mate."

"Where will you go now?"

"Back to Bedford. That's where Creighton and I hailed from, you know. I took his body there for burial."

"How is England, these days?"

"I wouldn't know, mate. I went back in time."

"Really? You did? You went back in time?"

"Right as rain, I did. The Boys Upstairs weren't having me on. They can do that. They can reverse the time-line."

"Why did you go back in time?"

"Creighton once told me, when he was in his cups, that he wanted to be buried in his family plot. There was a site set aside in the Bedford bone yard. I planted him there, with a grave marker."

"Was there any family on hand?"

"It was the dead of night, mate."

"Really? Why was that?"

"Well, it wouldn't do for me to be seen, would it?"

"Nope, I suspect not."

"The Boys Upstairs had already excavated the spot, so I deposited the coffin and the marker."

"All by yourself?"

"Nay, mate. I used the levitator."

"The levitator?"

"How do you fancy I moved all of those bags of cement? And how about the digital pianos? Those blighters are bloody heavy, you know."

"I never thought about it. But, please, go on."

"The Boys Upstairs filled in the hole. Then I said words over his remains and trundled off back here."

"Why didn't you stick around? You hadn't set foot in Jolly Old England for quite a while."

"The gravity, mate, the gravity. It was pushing me down. I wasn't accustomed to it, you see."

"Yeah, of course."

"And the air there wasn't as clean as it is here. Even though it was the nineteen-sixties, there'd been industry built up already. I was coughing my fool head off."

"But you said you were going to live in Bedford."

"I resolved to go to Bedford, as it existed in 1656."

"You can do that?"

"The Boys Upstairs said I could."

"Why 1656?"

"John Bunyan was preaching in Bedford then."

"John Bunyan? You mean the man who wrote *Pilgrim's Progress*?"

"The very same."

"He was a Bedford man?"

"Nay, mate. He was born and bred in Elstow. That's a few miles from Bedford. But he did some preaching in Bedford. And he was briefly jailed in Bedford."

"Jailed? Jailed for what?"

"He was a Puritan, wasn't he. And he was holding religious services, not in conformity with the C. of E., wasn't he. That was against the law in those days, wasn't it."

"The C. of E.?"

"Church of England, mate."

"Thanks. I forgot. Sorry."

"Anywise, I'd been hearing of this Bunyan bloke since I was a wee one. And he became a hero of mine. And so, I thought I'd like to see him and hear him in person, and mayhap chat him up a bit."

"And the Boys Upstairs are okay with that?"

"Why wouldn't they be?"

"I thought they might be afraid of affecting the time-space continuum."

Reginald harrumphed. "I don't know what that time-space nattering is about. But the Boys Upstairs didn't seem to be against the idea."

"Then it's fine. I wish you luck, my friend."

"Thanks."

"But won't you miss this place?"

"Nay, mate. I've had my fill of this Dale of the Dullards."

"Yeah, I suspect you have."

"I've been training my replacements."

"Replacements? Who's replacing you?"

"Do you bear in mind the blokes I told you about? The ones the Boys Upstairs had their eye on, before they hired Creighton and me?"

"Yeah."

"They're the ones filling in. I have them up to speed."

"Good for you."

"And you won't need their assistance for anything, if my guess is good. You haven't put in any orders, for more than a century now."

"Has it been that long?"

"By my calculation, give or take."

"Yeah, we colonists are getting by fine, with all the help you gave us, early on."

"I'd say as much."

"But one thing we learned, early on, is that we could get by without many possessions."

"A pearl of wisdom oft overlooked, that is."

"Yeah, the more things you own, the more headaches you have."

"Spot on, mate."

"One thing I'm curious about. And you've already made mention of it. But won't putting up with Earth's gravity be difficult for you?"

"For a bit it might. But I'll get used to it. And I'm going to be in Bedford for a day or so. No more than that."

"Where are you going when that's done?"

"That's it, mate. Bedford is the end of the line."

"You mean that you'll die in Bedford, after being there for a short visit?"

"There's no excuse for staying on any longer, is there?"

"Nope, I suspect not."

"The Boys Upstairs said I'll just evaporate. And it'll be painless. One sec, I'm in Bedford. Then nigh, I'm vapor."

"Uh, I don't know what to say."

"Well, you know, I've had a long life, mate. A very long life. And, like I said, I wanted to bid you cheery-bye, before I beetled off."

Craig extended his right hand.

Reginald took it and shook it.

"It's the end of an era," said Craig.

"And none too soon," said Reginald.

The electrician watched the filmmaker mount the camouflaged staircase and disappear.

"Goodbye, my friend," Craig said to the empty air. "May the past be everything you want it to be."

*****

Days later, on a visit to Earth Town, Craig arranged with George the Blacksmith and Orv the Mason to have a memorial tablet produced and placed at the entrance of Earth Town's system of gardens.

The inscription read: "To Creighton Beryl and Reginald Wylie, our chroniclers and help in times of need."

If anyone noticed the tablet, they made no mention of it to Craig.

*****

"It's the way of the world," said Andy, as he and Craig admired the tablet. "Good friends are rarely noticed, and easily forgotten."

"True that," Craig replied. "And more's the pity."

54—THE GOD WRITES

I take word processor in hand, one last time perchance, to record my thoughts. I sense the end coming. I know that sounds trite. But it's something I feel in my bones.

Three of the Earth Town founders remain above ground: Janis the Physician, Rance the Hunter, and Craig the Electrician.

I don't include myself as a founder, because I landed in the women's burg and didn't become a dweller of the plains until years afterward.

Although Earth Town lost people, it didn't lose their occupations. We still have a meat cutter, a butcher, a machinist, a blacksmith, a carpenter, a seamstress, a dentist, a farmer, a hunter, a baker, a cook, a horticulturalist, a mason, a mechanic, a plumber, a nurse, a justice of the peace, and a mayor. A few other job titles have since been stirred into the mix.

Janis retired as a physician long ago. But her trainees are on the job, both here and in the rainforest.

I say that Janis retired. But can a medical doctor ever retire? As long as a physician has a pulse and clear thinking, a healer remains a healer. People still come to Janis for advice on health matters.

Janis's protégé, Sheela, was the first indigenous medical doctor of Brook Haven in the Forest. And Sheela made it possible for every one of her sisters to become trained as a healer.

Sheela taught first-aid and anatomy and physiology in Gloria's day school. And so did the medicos who came after Sheela.

Since disease is still unknown to humans on this planet, much of a healer's life is spent in mending bones and ligaments and tendons and cuts and abrasions and bruises.

Otherwise, we're a healthy population. No one overeats. Our diets are high in fiber. There's no sucrose (table sugar). Everyone gets plenty of exercise, so indigestion isn't a problem. Neither do the humans here suffer from organic difficulties.

Even appendicitis and gall stones and kidney stones are rare. Sheela performed one appendectomy during her entire practice. And that was with Janis at her side.

When Sheela died, it was a great loss to her sisters. But the knowledge she dispensed over her lifetime lived on.

In fact, the forestland women's medical facility is named for her. They call it Sheela's Clinic.

Sheela's father (Mike the Horticulturalist) put flowers on the graves of Sheela and his wife, Nola, every time he visited his friends in Brook Haven in the Forest. He did this for hundreds of years.

Sadly, Mike had no relatives in Brook Haven in the Forest, since the Sorin line ran out with the death of his daughter, who never married.

Gloria is gone, too. But her school and sewing machines go on.

Craig set up a memorial plaque for Gloria at the school, where she had presided for centuries.

An art studio (abutting the school) and a library (near the bus stop) are also named for Gloria.

The library, founded by Gloria, is a concrete and air-conditioned edifice. It grew in size with each passing century. More than two thousand books are on its shelves. And a host of musical instruments are stored there, as protection against the malignant forces of nature.

The nightly campfire art-and-oratory performance is still called Gloria's Story Time.

And the archery range is called Gloria's Gallery.

The shy seamstress might have been a petite person, but she left a large and lasting legacy.

Rance the Hunter hasn't hunted in centuries. He doesn't even go fishing. He says his heart isn't in it. And when he says "it," he means "killing."

All of the Earth Town founders became vegetarians, after we'd been on this planet for a few hundred years. When there's no need to kill, there's no reason to kill—surely not for sport.

Craig the Electrician doesn't do electrical work, but that's because he has so many apprentices. He continues to jog every day, although he says it's more of a shuffle than true striding. And he still does pull-ups and chin-ups and push-ups and sit-ups and dips each morning. "It's a habit I can't seem to break," he tells me.

Janis says that nearly nine hundred years have passed since we found ourselves on this planet. It seems longer. I know that sounds like a joke. But it really isn't. People weren't meant to live this long—even people with a purpose.

Most of the original colonists stayed alive for eight hundred years; Ginger made it nearly that far. That's pretty good for a dog. She died at the funeral of her last pup. Her great and kind heart finally gave out.

Barney the Machinist was the first of the founders to go. He became wrinkled and gray. And he experienced joint pain, a few months before he died. But Barney was still active, right up until the end. In fact, he was weeding in one of the gardens, when he crumpled to the ground—never to rise again.

Then, one by one, the rest of them made their exits: Tim the Meat Cutter, Phil the Butcher, George the Blacksmith, Bailey the Carpenter, Chris the Farmer, Hank the Baker, Frank the Cook, Mike the Horticulturalist, Orv the Mason, Roy the Mechanic, Richie the Plumber, Dan the Dentist, Gloria the Seamstress, Linda the Justice of the Peace and Mayor, and Nancy the Nurse.

It's a curious thing. After a while, we tended to forget the surnames of our friends. Everyone was on a first-name basis, from the get-go.

The children born in Earth Town (Vik and Sluggo and Seth and Josh and Jon) survived a little past two hundred years. And they all passed on within a few months of each other.

The rainforest children predominantly live into their seventies, eighties, and nineties. They all die of old age. There have been no fatal accidents or illnesses. There's no disease here, yet, as far as anyone knows.

Dora died last year. This was quite a blow to all three municipalities in the valley. Dora had been a friend to everyone, no matter where they lived.

Of course, Dora's death hit her husband the hardest. Craig hasn't recovered, yet. He might never do so.

Can you imagine being married to someone for nine hundred years? I can't. I still mourn my wife, Zeena. And she died eight centuries ago.

We never figured out how or why Dora lived as long as she did. It's just one of the many mysteries on this mysterious planet.

Dora was widely perceived as "the mortal who became a deity"—almost a demigod, like Heracles. Dora enjoyed celebrity status. And she was celebrated and sought for her wisdom.

Although Dora was never chieftain, she (in addition to Gloria) was revered by the sisterhood. No chieftain ever made an exigent decision without consulting these ladies.

I was profoundly saddened by the passing of Koree, my co-pilot and fellow explorer—oh, so long ago. Koree and I came to be as close as two people of the opposite sex can be, without being married.

Koree was an occupant of both Earth Town and Brook Haven in the Forest, dividing her time between both communities. When Koree came out of retirement to take over the airline, she moved into Gloria's Quonset hut.

Whenever Koree was in Earth Town, she and I spent many lovely hours in each other's company. We sometimes worked in the gardens and orchards and vineyards and fields. We sometimes sat and drank coffee and dunked doughnuts in *Hank's and Frank's*. We sometimes walked around the Earth Town complex. All the time, we talked.

Koree did most of the talking. And I liked to listen to her. Koree was a lovely lady, and she had a quick mind.

Koree trained the *Albatross II* pilot (also a denizen of Brook Haven in the Forest) who took the reins from Koree, when Koree became too infirm to handle the shuttle.

In fact, to this day, every pilot of every airship, after Vik and Sluggo and me, has been a female from Brook Haven in the Forest. I didn't see that coming.

Over the years, I lent Koree library books I had read. And then, after she perused the literature, we talked about it. It was our own private book club.

The last I saw of Koree was when she visited Earth Town, as a passenger on the *Albatross II*. Koree knew she was dying, and she wanted to be with me one more time.

When I heard of Koree's death, a day later, I broke down. I didn't go outside for a week. It felt as bad as when I lost Zeena.

Gloria chiseled an epitaph into the two biggest rocks in Koree's Sacred Knoll cairn. It says: "She faced her fear and went above and beyond."

True that.

I didn't go to Koree's memorial service at Brook Haven in the Forest. It would've been too much for me.

The Earth Town society attached a cenotaph to the front door of Koree's Quonset hut. It says: "Koree: Pilot, explorer, artist, seamstress, and friend."

We had a memorial service for Koree in Earth Town. I showed up for it. But, when they asked me to say something, I wasn't able to talk. I had to walk away.

I couldn't cope with my grief. It took me another week before I could speak to anyone, without breaking down.

They say it's a mistake to get too close to people, because it hurts so much when they leave. I know now that this is oh-so-very true.

I visit Koree's cenotaph every day and pat it tenderly. Each week, Craig puts flowers in front of Koree's cairn in the Sacred Knoll—in my name.

Craig still resides in the same thatched hut which he shared with his wife in Brook Haven in the Forest. I still make his Earth Town Quonset hut my home.

It amazes me that these Quonset huts have stood for so long. Whatever material our benefactors used to devise them—it's superior stuff.

Earth Town's compound is now several times its nascent size—which consisted of (in the first year) a circle of Quonset huts, a threshing floor, and a corral for the goats and antelope.

Earth Town's gardens, orchards, vineyards, fields of grain, and refrigerated storehouses and dairies are, in a word, expansive. Negotiating the footpath to the farthest grove takes me a good twenty minutes. And that's at a brisk pace.

On the far side of the vineyard, we plant our dead. In the early years, the Earth Town citizens didn't see the need for a graveyard. Nowadays, the flatland necropolis is pocked with headstones—quarried and lugged from our cultivated acreage.

Although I have resided in Earth Town for centuries, I prefer to be laid to rest in the Sacred Knoll of the rainforest. I have made it known, to those in charge of such matters, that I want to be interred near Zeena and Koree. In the lyrics of an old cowboy song: "Bury me not on the lone prairie."

The seminal library still stands. But a second library (a much larger concrete construction) is where most of the books and musical instruments are kept.

Movie nights are no longer held in the old library. Centuries ago, a film theater and an amphitheater (for stage productions and musical performances) were erected. We've come a long way from a few rows of folding chairs and a projector and a collapsible screen.

We have a special structure in Earth Town; it's called the Pentagon—because the building has five sides to it. Each indoor facet of the Pentagon is dedicated to an explored island on this planet. And the walls feature the framed artwork (rendered by Vik and Sluggo and Koree) of the flora and fauna of each isle.

This is where I do my writing. I frequently have privacy, because the Pentagon is rarely visited. And that's a shame, because the artwork is excellent. It unerringly depicts the animals and plants I saw.

People ask me how the artists could put in such detail, since we were scudding above these islands in the *Albatross II*. But they forget that we were gliding around, so we could see these specimens from all sides. And Vik and Sluggo and Koree touched up and colored in their drawings (based on their memories and the notes I took) on our return.

I don't credit my flying abilities, such as they are. It's that I had competent and imaginative artists working with me. And it is to these three people that the Pentagon is fittingly dedicated.

In the middle of the Pentagon is a bookcase containing the many volumes of the tome I began composing centuries ago. This literature has been consistently supplemented, since I typed the first sentence of it on a word processor, oh-so-long-ago. Janis jokingly calls the book "our story—our Bible." And some people see it as holy writ. But I prefer Craig's title: *Andy's Annals*.

Viewing it as a Bible is a bit of a stretch. But I suppose all historians see their work as being sacred, in a way. My prayer is that a religion isn't created in my name, after I'm gone. That type of thing occasionally happened on Earth.

Brook Haven in the Forest grew, too. More thatched huts were patched together. The garden and goat pen got bigger. The cemetery (once called the Place of Seven Graves, and later termed the Sacred Knoll) is magnified far beyond its inceptive size.

I was unsure where the excavators found rocks to cover each plot in the Sacred Knoll. It turns out, according to Craig, that the ground already contained them. Each time the women dug a grave, plenty of rocks were unearthed. You might say the Sacred Knoll is a natural spot for a cairn necropolis.

I never went back to Brook Haven in the Forest, which we once called Zeena's Village. I couldn't see a reason for it.

I never returned to the islands I once explored, either. I doubt whether much has changed on those earthen hunks sticking out of the briny sea. Nine hundred years is a spit in the ocean, compared to geological time.

The *Albatross II* is alive and kicking. Most, if not all, of its original parts have been replaced, though. In this respect, it's like a conundrum the ancient Athenians tackled: When the Ship of Perseus was restored, plank by plank, over many years—at what point did it cease being the Ship of Perseus? The philosophers never came to an agreement on that.

The *Albatross II* was, centuries later, joined by the *Albatross III*, since we had so many people constantly commuting between Earth Town and Brook Haven in the Forest.

I used the *Albatross II* to explore the planet. But I only got as far as two islands on either side of this island—five isles in all. I didn't foresee the craft's present and more practical use, as a shuttle between two neighborhoods. But that worked out just fine. And I'm glad of it.

Population control in Earth Town and Brook Haven in the Forest didn't pose a problem. Most couples had one or two children. They were, in essence, replacing themselves.

It wasn't exactly Planned Parenthood. It's just the way things occurred. Perchance it was set up by our benefactors to be this way. No one knows. Or, if they do know, they're not talking.

Racial discrimination was perpetually an issue. The fisher folk are still sending the occasional light-skinned infant girl to Brook Haven in the Forest and the occasional light-skinned infant boy to Earth Town. In the beginning, light skin was seen as a curse. Now, it's seen as a boon—a way out of want and ignorance. But it's racism, nevertheless.

The fisher folk have yet to evolve in any significant way. They live as they did a millennium ago. They subsist, but they never advance.

The fisher folk were, and continue to be, afraid of change. And I sympathize with their plight. Change can be difficult. It can be painful. But it's the key to progress. You can't get anywhere by staying in one spot.

The fisher folk see how their children thrive in Brook Haven in the Forest, and they're proud of them. The girls learn drawing, music, and a plethora of skills—besides being educated to read and write and do arithmetic and practice the healing arts.

The fisher folk don't visit Earth Town. For one thing, it's a two-day walk. More to the point, though, they're too ashamed to see the males they abandoned. At least, that's the scuttlebutt in the rainforest.

This sounds to me like a double standard. But who am I to judge?

One of my pet projects was to chart the night sky. I had assistance from generations of boys who manned the telescope in the evenings and aided me in mapping the constellations and their movements.

The woodland girls decided they wanted a telescope, too. And, as usual, they got what they wanted. But the girls turned out to be a big help with my project, so no one complained.

We found other planets and moons, which roughly corresponded to what the skies of Earth showed me. As for identifying the stars in this planet's heavens, I never found a way to do it. I'm quite likely light years across the spiral galaxy from my former home. And I might not be seeing any of the stars I saw on Earth.

But we did confirm that five satellites, probably artificial, hang high above each of the islands I explored. And they seem to be in geosynchronous orbits. Why the satellites are there, I can only conjecture.

I asked Craig if he would talk to his documentarian pals about this. He says he did, but they're as much in the dark as we are. Craig claims that Creighton and Reginald, as well as their replacements, Bud and Lou, never cared about such considerations.

Craig and I recently conversed about the meaning of life. Craig says that meaning is like perfection: You can never reach it. But life can become more meaningful—provided one is constantly learning and getting closer to the truth of things and doing good work and meeting deadlines and achieving goals and coming through for others and pleasing oneself.

Life also becomes more meaningful as we personally grow—as we become nicer and more understanding and more merciful and more just and fair in our dealings. If we become happier and stay happy, on this road of ethical self-improvement, that's icing on the cake. But happiness is not something to seek; it's something to find.

Craig is convinced that there's no Afterlife.

"Why would there be one?" he posited. "You and I already know what it's like to live forever. Or what seems like forever. We had a lengthy life, in two worlds.

"Length doesn't equal meaning," Craig went on. "A lengthy life isn't necessarily a reward.

"And why would there be an unending Afterlife Paradise without pain or care? Such a life would have no meaning.

"That's something the ancient Greeks understood. Because mortal life is brief, it's precious. Conversely, a life with no end is devoid of substance.

"The Greek gods of Olympus weren't creators. They, themselves, were created.

"But, because the Olympic gods knew they would live forever, they had no ethics or morals. They did whatever they wanted to do, because there was no blowback. Zeus was unfaithful to Hera several times. But if vengeance was ever visited upon him, it was in those few circumstances when Hera found him out. Then, Hera punished him, as only a wife can.

"But mortals don't enjoy such luxury. People have ethics and morals, because they know everything will end for them someday. And a Judgment on High might follow. But a judgment by their peers, and history, is a certainty.

"You and I have survived far longer than the normal span. But we shall die, either by accident or old age.

"The Hebrews had a phrase for it: *Mot toomoot* (You will die).

"The Romans said: *Memento mori* (Keep in mind that you will die) and *Sic gloria transit* (Fame is fleeting).

"Knowing that death is inescapable is what gives life significance.

"Although most humans would be tickled to death, if they thought they could live forever, immortality would be frivolous. If you lived forever, nothing would matter in the end. In fact, there would be no end. Instead, because you're mortal, every moment is momentous."

I couldn't agree more.

Now, I'd like to set the record straight about something. I keep telling people: "I'm not a deity"—even though the fisher folk still refer to me as the God in the Sky. I'll never live that down. And it's my own fault.

I didn't set out to be a god. It just happened. And it seemed to work to my advantage. So, I let people think what they wanted.

Kurt Vonnegut wrote: "We are what we pretend to be, so we must be careful about what we pretend to be."

I pretended to be a beneficent deity. And I was cautious about it. I didn't abuse the trappings. I probably did some good.

I never claimed to be a god. If I sinned in this respect, it was a sin of omission. I let people believe what they wanted to believe—which they would do, anyway.

It doesn't help that my hair and beard have whitened—and I let them grow longer. Craig says I resemble Michelangelo's deity depicted on the ceiling of the Sistine Chapel.

One day, we'll all be gone. By "we," I mean the sons and daughters of the gods, the mighty men and women that were of old.

Because of my writings, we might be remembered. But one never can tell. Writings have ways of becoming altered, lost, or shunted aside.

What will this planet be like in another millennium? Will the succeeding relatives of Earthling transplants learn from our successes and mistakes? Will they make this world a better place?

Or will they spill out of this valley and despoil this Eden? Will they burst the trial balloon of our benefactors? Will they trash this planet like our Earthling contemporaries trashed their planet? Will they make war instead of love?

My Earthling generation was supposed to fix the errors committed by our parents. We were supposed to make everything on Earth all right again. But we made things worse—far worse.

Will that be the fate of this planet? Are we humans doomed to imprudence and mediocrity, no matter what?

One last matter: I don't know where the Glittering Gods came from. Would they necessarily have to be from Earth, since Earth is the only place in the universe where life can be sustained? Did they evolve from Earth's chaotic and murky beginnings?

This seems logical, providing I have all the facts. But do I have all the facts? I don't know.

So, there you have it.

I'm going to shut down the word processor now and go outside and sit in the sun. It's my favorite thing to do, as of late.

If this is my final communication, let me conclude it by saying: Be well, do good work, and keep in touch with those you love.

That's a pretty good prescription for life—no matter how long, or short, your life is.

Oh, yes. And let me add: Eat or drink something sweet, every day. It couldn't hurt. And it might help.

It helped me.

OTHER BOOKS BY BRUCE PIERCE

MYSTERY SERIES

The Dunbar Curse

The Turner Tragedy

An Artistic Death

Lest We Forget

The Million-Dollar Medallion

Hit and Miss

SHORT STORY COLLECTIONS

The Marsha Chronicles

The Huge Farewell

WESTERN

The Angel of Death

SCIENCE FICTION

Whateley Island

Bad is Coming

The Weather Man

NON-FICTION

The Lesser-Read Bible

What Makes Brucie Run?

What Makes Brucie Golf?

What Else Makes Brucie Golf?

ABOUT THE AUTHOR

Bruce Pierce spent his childhood in rural Minnesota and attended big-city colleges and universities and graduate schools. He worked all sorts of jobs and did all kinds of things. But he never grew up. And he tends to spin outlandish yarns. Bruce and his wife, Sherry, are residents of Laveen, Arizona.

www.ingramcontent.com/pod-product-compliance
Lightning Source LLC
LaVergne TN
LVHW010539160826
845677LV00013B/2932

* 9 7 9 8 4 0 6 2 4 5 4 9 1 *